almost gone

Brian Sousa

almost gone

A NOVEL IN STORIES

Tagus Press · UMass Dartmouth · Dartmouth, Massachusetts

FOR MY GRANDFATHER,
JOAQUIM HENRIQUES DE SOUSA,
AND MY PARENTS

—

PORTUGUESE IN THE AMERICAS SERIES, 20
Tagus Press at UMass Dartmouth
www.portstudies.umassd.edu
© 2013 The University of Massachusetts Dartmouth
All rights reserved
Manufactured in the United States of America
General Editor: Frank F. Sousa
Managing Editor: Mario Pereira
Designed by Mindy Basinger Hill
Typeset in Calluna

Tagus Press books are produced and distributed for Tagus Press
by University Press of New England, which is a member
of the Green Press Initiative. The paper used in this book meets
their minimum requirement for recycled paper.

For all inquiries, please contact:
Tagus Press at UMass Dartmouth
Center for Portuguese Studies and Culture
285 Old Westport Road
North Dartmouth MA 02747-2300
Tel. 508-999-8255
Fax 508-999-9272
www.portstudies.umassd.edu

"One Last Thing" appeared in *Gávea-Brown* 26–27 (2005–6): 104–13
and is reprinted by permission of Gávea-Brown Publications.

"Plastic Chairs" and "Just One Night" appeared in *Verdad, a Journal of Literature
and Art* in 2012, and are reprinted courtesy of www.verdadmagazine.org.

Library of Congress Cataloging-in-Publication Data

Sousa, Brian.
Almost gone: a novel in stories / Brian Sousa.
p. cm. — (Portuguese in the Americas series; 20)
ISBN 978-1-933227-45-0 (pbk.: alk. paper)
1. Portuguese—United States—Fiction. I. Title.
PS3619.O877A79 2013
813'.6—dc23   2012033962

5   4   3   2   1

contents

foreword

BY FRANK X. GASPAR

Almost Gone — an important debut novel from a leading member of a new generation of Portuguese-American writers — is a tough, many-layered story that arises from the tough, many-layered lives of its characters, moving forward and backward in staccato grace between generations and their deeper drives and anxieties. Sousa's technique is apt in his approach to the weaving of this novel, for something of this scope could swell and curve like the complicated masterworks of Balzac or Trollope or Eça de Queirós, but we live in a different age, and in *Almost Gone*, time is fragmented as we experience it, and we come to know the characters not in the unbroken arc of classic development but in fragments of story, each piece adding and connecting until a tremulous whole begins to emerge, and we experience a circle of fated persons living in their presents and alive also in their pasts, spanning the Lusophone globe from Portugal to Rhode Island to Brazil. It is a circle that will implode upon itself, of course, and this is Sousa's design.

At the novel's center is Scott, a third-generation Portuguese American. There is something biblical in the way Scott seemingly inherits a darkness from the generations before him, such as from his grandfather Nuno, who came to America, as so many immigrants have, hauling a heavy cordage of secrets and conflicts along with him, and as we touch the lives of others in the Portuguese community — and in far-flung settings in Europe and South America, too — we gain a sense of the connections, sometimes deep and sometimes tenuous, between the young Scott, his father, his grandfather and grandmother, other fathers, wives, and children, and a somewhat mysterious and alluring neighbor. We are, in the course of the novel, given privilege to the interlocking difficulties of a family that might seem, if we knew them but slightly, well assimilated into American mainstream culture. But Sousa does not treat them casually, nor does he fall into the trap of a clichéd immigrant rags-to-riches narrative (though Nuno and his extended family clearly have achieved the comforts of the solid working-class). What Sousa does is to allow the reader to experience their darker moments and their particular struggles, and we feel in each of them the urge to find some sort of solace and sense in a world of challenges that they are not always equal to.

It would do disservice to the book to speak in more particulars than I have here, for *Almost Gone* offers its share of revelations and surprises. Suffice it to say that Sousa shrinks from nothing and that his characters are sometimes shocking and sometimes strangely familiar. What lies buried in the heart and what will out is the engine driving all these pieces. Part of the gravity of the book emanates from the way the chapters early on resemble discrete stories, arcing seemingly unto themselves—but then they begin deftly and inexorably crossing and melding into a rich and richly unsettling surface that yields to the attentive reader deeply not only the Portuguese-American experience but also the unique darknesses and driving hopes of a clutch of human hearts. *Almost Gone* is a book for all Portuguese and Portuguese-American readers—one might say a *necessary* book, for it affirms the presence of a segment of Portuguese-American life so far ignored—but it is also a book for all readers, for it touches on the universal and common struggles of the heart: it is a book that will meet a part of everyone, regardless of cultural background or ethnic identity. Sousa has broken ground here—a sometimes dark and brooding psychic landscape, to be sure, but the earth he has turned over is rich, dark, and redolent of whole worlds past, present, and future. There is happiness in the thought that this is a debut novel, and that we can expect further exploration of these worlds—and we can look forward to readers taking part in the fictional lives of Portuguese-Americans, who are perhaps no more mysterious than anyone else. And no less, either.

almost gone

fortaleza

SCOTT · 2010

Each morning I awaken to the cheers of children as they slide down dunes on pieces of cardboard. I roll off my sagging mattress, scrub my hands under the brownish water in the cracked sink in the corner and look through the open window of the small room. The sand flies flit and buzz around me. I've disturbed them. The children are far too skinny here. The sharp bones of their elbows and shoulder blades press painfully against their skin. They take turns, landing in a cloud at the bottom, shaking the sand from their ears and hair and shoving each other as they run back to the top.

I scratch the row of lumped bug bites on my chest, and then my hand stays on my stomach. It's flat and tight. I used to dream of McDonald's and Burger King commercials at night, of pushing mushy burgers into my mouth so fast I could choke on them. The way you used to when you were really hungry, Emily.

"Slow down," Hailey would warn you. "Slow down."

But I don't need the things that I once thought I did. We don't really *need* things, I guess. Television, newspapers, breakfast cereals, new clothes. They're all worthless. I eat what I can when I'm hungry. I swim when I'm hot. I wasn't even jerking off much until I met Fernanda. She could be something. I think she could be something. What does it matter how old she is? No one here cares. At first I got a lot of "Hey, *gringo*, why you here?" People used to constantly ask me for money because I'm white and I'm from the States, but they've given up. My cash will be gone soon, anyway. Before I left I transferred half of our savings to Banco Central do Brasil, but it's really not that much. It's lasted because I only spend it on food and booze.

I'm thinking that I'll try to sell coconuts on the beach when my money runs out. I've seen local men scale up the palms in the early morning, cutting down the fruit with machetes so it thuds in the sand. I think I could do that.

When I first arrived in Rio de Janeiro, the chaos assaulted me: the manic honking and squealing tires, the crowded sidewalks where businessmen with wet, carefully combed hair walk alongside beggars with missing hands and arms. The city made me jumpy, skittish; I couldn't stay there. Here, by the beach in Fortaleza, I can fade away among the fishermen, peddlers and drug dealers — and while they don't accept me, they know I'm not a threat. Sometimes I think they can see right through me, that they know why I'm here, but I'm probably just being paranoid.

The tourists are the only group that I still hide from. There aren't as many vacationers and backpackers here as there were in Rio, but they still find their way to the beach from time to time. They drink beer and sit out on the *pousada* veranda smoking and laughing. They're so anxious to swim and drink and fuck that it's written on their puffy red faces, and I ignore their questions about scoring drugs and prostitutes unless I think I can make a quick buck off a recommendation. If they're American, they comment on the weathered Red Sox hat that I wear, the one that I bring with me everywhere.

Today the veranda is empty. I walk barefoot through the hot sand and stop next to a rusted Volkswagen to stare at my reflection. My hat is jammed down on my head, and my eyes are still swollen underneath the tattered brim. Under my eyebrows the skin is crusty and yellowed. They've been like this for two days now. I must be allergic to something.

Before the sun gets too hot and the air too wet, the mornings here are empty. The crisp breeze off Praia de Iracema, the old men sipping *café* at small white tables, reading the morning's *Diário do Nordeste*. It almost feels hopeful. But you never leave my mind, Emily. I can hear you exhale with every step I take. You're always up on my shoulders, where you loved to sit, your hands buried in my hair, your swinging weight pressing down on me. You flash in the dull eyes of stray dogs that pass by, and float in the wet steam of the sickly sweet *café* served in short Styrofoam cups that I buy on the street in the mornings for half a *real*.

At the *farmácia*, I show the man the swelling around my eyes, and he wordlessly hands me a package of white pills that I don't recognize. At the market I buy bananas, a pack of cigarettes, and two large bottles of water for two *real* and walk back to the *pousada*. A young beggar is lying in the shade of the palms in front of the hostel, his tan stomach bloated. Balanced on his chest is a bottle of rum. His arms are disproportionably stubby.

"*Obrigado,*" he mutters, holding out a blackened palm, thanking me before I've given him anything.

I told Fernanda I'd meet her at the beach later, so I have several hours to kill. She's studying English in school, and I know Spanish pretty well and a few words in Portuguese, so we get by. The Portuguese they speak here is different than the way my grandfather used to speak, though. I remember the sound of my dad and my grandfather talking on the sidelines of the soccer fields when I was a kid, the way their voices stood out from the others and grew amplified as the game went on. It was only when he was really excited or angry that my dad would slip back into it, and it used to embarrass me when I'd hear *"Centro! Centro! Pasa, Scott!"* Afterward they'd each hug me tightly and kiss me on the cheek, but I'd duck away so no one could see.

In my room I pull down the blinds and reach under the mattress to feel for the slit. I stuff my money in and take out two Oxys—Hailey's from when she had back surgery last year. I make sure that the key to the room is still tied around my neck, and then sit out on the veranda with the plastic bag from the market, my bottle of rum, and the cheap pocket knife I bought on the street in Rio. The ashtray is overflowing with cigarette butts and I push it away, eat two bananas and drink half of one of the bottles of water. The allergy pills taste sour going down, they are bigger than I thought, and I have trouble swallowing them. I wash them down with two long pulls of rum. I've been snorting the Oxys because I want to make them last. I know I can find drugs on the street here, but they won't be anything like these. Methodically, I cut one—in the middle so none is wasted—and then grind it until the pieces are small and fine. I use the back of the knife to scrape out four lines, and use a shiny paper *real* to snort them up. It barely burns anymore.

After the first rush, I light a cigarette and sit for a while, waiting for that feeling of white-washed numbness, when my mind goes almost entirely blank and Emily goes to sleep.

An hour or so later I walk down the treaded paths in the dunes to Praia de Futuro, a slab of shallow water glowing green. Naked children run circles around shallow tide pools where horse shoe crabs and sea urchins float listlessly. They say it has been a dry year here in eastern Brazil, but I wouldn't have anything to compare it to.

I sit in the shade, but it's hot as hell and my eyes are burning and itching, so I tentatively make my way to the water. When I dunk my head, I force open my eyes and they sting furiously in the salt, but then begin to feel better. I start the long swim out to the sandbar, pushing against the incoming tide, waving to a small fishing skiff that floats by on its way out. The two men are arguing with each other, and one glares at me, holding a fishing net in one hand. He points to his own eyes and yells something to me in Portuguese, shaking his finger. I nod and keep swimming, and both of the men explode into laughter as they kick on the engine and diesel fumes fill the air.

My feet finally touch firm sand. The swim isn't too bad, maybe two hundred yards or so, and the waves are usually gentle. But today the tide is rougher, with a strong undertow. When I'm waist deep I slick back my hair and then wash my hands repeatedly in the water, rubbing them together. I'm breathing harder than usual, and a strange dizziness has seized me. Behind me, back over the swells, the beach is framed by walls of red dunes. Up over the dunes are the sandy alleys and streets that eventually lead to the city of Fortaleza, where Fernanda is from. It really does look like paradise out here, and sometimes I feel like I should be sending postcards to people—my dad, my mother, Hailey. But I don't think I ever will. After it happened, dad was barely able to talk to me. My mother suggested I get therapy. "Mental illness runs in the family on your father's side," she once said quietly, glancing gravely across the dinner table. My stomach heaved when she said it. I knew she was talking about my grandmother. But she was also talking about me, and I saw that little fucking nod of agreement from Hailey—that smug flick of her head. I couldn't take it. The last thing I told my father was that I was going away for a while.

I didn't kill you or leave you to die, but you know that, Emily. You were dying in the hospital, scared as hell, and all I did was fulfill your last wish. I let you go happily, in my arms. What I did was right. It was what you wanted. That thought is what gets me through every day: each hung-over, burning morning, each weightless, silent swim I take in the afternoon.

I'm floating on my back in the shallow water, the way my father showed me to when I was young, trying not to doze off, when I hear splashing. A boy smiles as he wades past me onto the sandbar. I didn't even see him swim out. He looks to be around eleven or twelve but he's already almost my height, with a lean, ropy frame. He's breathing rapidly and tugging at the bottoms of his cut-off jean shorts.

I'm usually alone at this spot during the middle of the day, swimming and diving under to cool my parched skin. Most of the locals don't bother to swim out so far. They don't need to escape the heat the way I do. Squinting in the glinting sun, I duck my head under and then look back at the boy. I don't want to share this with him. His smile shines yellow compared to the bright white of his eyes.

"*Oi,*" I say.

He nods his head, still smiling, slapping his palms in the water. I feel my heart pounding now, faster than usual. I'm still waist deep, the cool water swirling gently around me, but why do I feel so faint? My skin itches and crawls, as if hot and cold hands are running up and down my back.

I'm fine, I tell myself. I'm fine. I stumble a little in the water as my head spins. "Jesus Christ," I say, "what the fuck."

He is watching me now, laughing and standing up, the water around his knees. "Fuck," he mimics excitedly, "Jesus Christ."

"Yeah," I say, and swing my head back toward shore. Everything is slowing down, and I'm not sure my voice is audible anymore. My breathing is coming hard and fast. A reaction to the medication? I know I should climb up on the sand next to the boy, maybe lie down where it is most shallow, but instead I concentrate on standing still. My body feels like it did that morning in college, after the night I tried cocaine for the first time. My body is vibrating and my knees want to buckle, but if I can just withstand the rush of nerves and weakness, the trembling, I'll make it.

The boy is staring at me expectantly, crouching down with his hands on his knees. What does he want? What the hell is happening? I know one thing. I need to swim back. A rush of blood fills me and the thought of getting back to shore and climbing onto the hot sand energizes me. Water. Shade. Rum. I point toward shore, and the boy nods and waves at me in slow motion.

I wave back and flash him the thumbs-up sign as I slide into deeper water. I've done this swim hundreds of times. The water wraps around my neck, and I start to swim smoothly and as calmly as I can, taking deep breaths that just barely ache in my lungs. God, I shouldn't smoke so much.

My energy fades in about a minute, though, and I feel sluggish. The strong, slow-building swells push me toward the distant shore, and at some point I close my eyes so I can concentrate on digging my hands into the water that is thicker now, heavier. I'll turn when I need to breathe. I can float if I need to. I must be getting close. I kick my legs and lift my head but the beach still looks far away. Maybe it's shallow here? Maybe there's a rock or a reef, something below me to stand on?

But my legs scramble, and my feet flail and touch nothing but emptiness. My hands open and close, my arms spin frantic circles, and suddenly I feel cool water rushing into my lungs as I choke and cough, slapping my hands against the water as the boy did. I can't breathe this air, but for some reason pulling my head up is too difficult. I want to press it further and further down into the cold, to sink down and rest.

Suddenly I am flipped over. The sun blinks on and I gasp and retch, the taste of bananas and rum hot in my mouth, then sticky on my chest. There is a hand digging into the small of my back, and above me I see the boy's pink, open mouth and wet black hair. An arm curled around my neck. As he pulls me, I hear him jabbering in Portuguese, but I still can't move my arms or my legs as he slowly drags me across the surface.

The sky flashes blue above me and the boy is tugging hard, but we don't seem to be moving. I can't feel my arms. How far are we from shore? Why the hell can't I move my legs? I close my eyes and choke and see you, Emily, climbing onto my shoulders so I can run around the house with you again and again. Hailey's laughing from the kitchen, yelling "Be careful, be careful!" I feel my heart chugging slowly, but Emily, your feet are pressing me down and I'm sinking into the blackness again—should I let myself go? My eyes sting in the salt and the sun, I feel his hands pressing down—*but why down? why pressing down?*—on my chest and then my shoulders, and my eyes flash open as I flail my arms and kick, and with my last bit of strength I grip his skull as I go under, gasping, choking, and then pull him under me, my fingers clutching at his open mouth, Emily's hand pushing too, her face flashing above me, my knees digging into his back, one of his arms pressing my throat, then air filling my lungs.

Floating on my back, coughing and spitting. My strength beginning to return, the sun feverish above me.

I gasp and tread water weakly and wait for the boy to pop up. I can't focus my eyes. My hands flap in the sunshine, but I'm too far out for people to see. Spin around and around, looking for the boy's head, his kicking feet. I don't see anything. Wait, did he swim in already? He must have. Is he mixed into that crowd of brown bodies clustered around the shore? I open my eyes underwater and see nothing, then begin to slowly drag myself toward the shore, my arms aching, spitting blood from my mouth, until I'm sure I can stand. As I get closer, I can feel their eyes on me. Where is he? Did he tell everyone about me? I stagger and pick my way through the bathers. My knee is red and swollen. The beach is blurry and the rocky sand stings my feet.

But I've made it. I pull my legs up under my arms, sit down against a palm tree, and throw up between my legs. Two older women, one blonde, one brunette, are sunbathing topless on their backs, their brown breasts slumping to the sides. I wonder if they saw what happened. I watch as the one on the right, who has short, curly black hair and wears aviator sunglasses, sits up groggily and murmurs something to the other while scanning the shoreline. She catches me looking and glares at me as she takes a drag of her cigarette, then puts it out in the sand. Both women turn onto their stomachs in unison.

I sit there and stare at the water, waiting, wondering. The sand grows hot under me, my skin and shorts dry out. I'm dying for a drink and my head is cloudy and heavy, but I just let it hang there, my chin on my chest.

I'm awakened by a tap on my shoulder. How long was I asleep?

The boy is sitting next to me in the sand. His eyes are gleaming green in the center and his hair is wet.

I breathe a sigh of relief and touch his shoulder with my hand. *"Obrigado,"* I say. *"Muito obrigado."*

He smiles at me and holds out his hand expectantly.

But I have nothing to give him right now. I could bring him up to my room, give him a few *real*. But then he might see where I keep everything.

"Obrigado," I say again, but when he shoves his open hand at me, I push it away. He shrugs, gets up, and jogs down the beach, but I don't feel ready to stand up.

⌣

In my room I run my hands under the water in the sink, and then pour some rum into a plastic cup. There is no ice. I sit on the floor and lean against the wall.

I know that I drink so I don't think of you, Emily. I understand that. When my mind is clear, usually in the early morning as I awaken, all the thin bones in my face aching, I psychoanalyze. Why I left, why I've stayed here. The mornings are the only times that my mind, almost against my will, works over what went down at the beach that day. Hailey, my father, the police; everyone told me that what I claim happened is impossible. But I remember you running into the water, calling out goodbye. Before I walked out of her office, Dr. Rich said that when people are in shock they distort memories that they can't face. That's not what happened. But the last time I tried to tell Hailey *my* version, her face drained of color, and she ignored me. Instead, she asked if I'd gotten what I wanted. I couldn't look at her after that, much less listen to her.

In each stale morning I arrive at the same three conclusions. I know what I saw. I did nothing wrong. And no one will ever believe me. It didn't matter to me that when I went to the children's hospital to pay the bills that we owed, the nurse wouldn't speak to me, and one doctor threatened to take me out to the parking lot and whip my ass. I didn't care. But it disgusted and scared me when I got the distinct feeling that underneath it all, Hailey wasn't as upset as she was pretending to be. I don't think she really misses you, Emily. And I hate to say it, baby, but I'm not sure Hailey ever loved you like I did. Like I do.

I drink the first glass fast, and you don't fade as you do with the second and the third; instead, you become whole. Real. I remember your small hands and the way they dug into my back when I swung you around, your skinny legs dangling in the air. I think a lot about decisions, about when I was a kid. How one night with Hailey five years ago—in my parents' bed when they were away for the weekend—changed everything. We hadn't used a condom; we'd always been stupid like that, so lost in the feel of each other, the thrill of it. I kept telling Hailey I'd pull out before I came, and when I tried to, jerking backward, she pushed forward and pulled me into her, her hands on my hips. And you know what, Emily? Lying there afterward, I could feel your presence already.

With two drinks in me, I lean my head back. My neck and shoulders start to relax, and my life feels as though it is split cleanly into two: Before and After. Before, I lived in Rhode Island three streets away from my parents with my wife and our child. Before, I taught English and coached the soccer team at my old high school. After, my child grew ill with leukemia and my marriage got completely fucked up. After, my daughter drowned at our favorite beach, as I slept on the shore twenty feet from her. Before and After. But I am able to look at these two sides of myself from some type of fleeting distance, the taste of rum sweet on my lips.

With three drinks I close my eyes and hear the scrape of a gray plane across a blue sky. My life stops rewinding, and my parents and my grandparents and Hailey begin to disappear, their voices barely whispering in my ears. Sometimes, waking up, the voices are loud, a raspy mix of Portuguese and English, and I don't know if they're outside the window or inside my head. But in the quiet room, with the salt breeze through the window and my bare feet extended before me, they grow faint.

My four-drink daydream is that you will appear here, Emily. It seems only right. You'll find me on the beach sleeping and curl up next to me, warm and happy, and we will begin our new life.

—

Fernanda and I have planned to meet at one of the marinas at the outskirts of the city, near Porto das Dunas, right down the street from where we first met. I'd been sitting in a dive bar drinking *caipirinhas*, a drink they make here with ground lemon, sugar, and the grain alcohol *cachaca*, which the locals call *pinga*. That day I went out on the street to smoke and stared, unabashed, as a group of girls from the high school walked by. Fernanda lingered as the rest of the group pointed and screeched their way down the street, and then she approached me and casually asked for a cigarette. I was suddenly too shy to look directly at her face, but when I did, she was looking right at me, her eyeshadow glittering silver. I realized I'd seen her on the beach before, that I'd tried to not watch the way her young body shook and moved as she ran into the water.

We've spent a lot of time together over the last few weeks, probably too much. I was cautious at first, but no one here seems to care that she's fifteen—not her friends, not the bartenders. We haven't made love, haven't even come close. A few days ago she led me around the streets of the city, pointing out her high school, her house. She bought a *pastel* for me, and then kissed me while the thin crumbs stuck to my lips, her mouth closed and then half open. I don't know what she sees in me, whether I am exotic with my dirty-blond hair and fair skin or what, but today I showered in the dirty communal bathroom at the hostel and smeared on the last of my melted deodorant. I shaved the scruffy beard that I've been growing and brushed my teeth and my tongue roughly to try to get rid of the taste of rum. I do know that when I'm with Fernanda, Emily doesn't come to me. And as guilty as I sometimes feel, I like knowing that while we're together, I'm freer than I've been in a while.

I smoke and spit into the water as I wait for her. I can still see the dunes and the beach, but now I'm closer to the heart of the city, the hotels, the universities, all the normal stuff that I try to stay away from. Just when I begin to feel claustrophobic, I see her. She's wearing tight jeans and a pink T-shirt that ends above her stomach, and her long black hair is pulled back with a yellow tie. It's impossible to see unless I'm up close to her, but her forehead is covered in tiny pimples. I felt them, small and hard, when I brushed her hair away from her face the last time.

We hug and kiss hello on each cheek, and my face burns. The swelling has gone down a little, but she furrows her brow and touches gingerly around each of my eyes. "*Alergia?*" she asks, sniffling.

I shrug. "Are you okay? What's the matter?" I ask.

She shakes her head and leads me to the edge of the dock. We sit down next to each other, and I offer her my hand.

"My brother," she says haltingly, examining my palm with damp fingers, "My brother not. Came?"

"Come."

She shakes her head and smiles, embarrassed. "Come back."

I've never met her brother, or her parents, and don't really feel the need to. I stare down at her hands. Her nails, short and chipped, are one of the things that remind me how young she is. She bites them.

"He go to *praia com minha mãe*. But not come today," she says more confidently, and leans against me. When her body touches me, I'm instantly aroused, and that doesn't happen that much anymore. Even when I see the women sunbathing on the beach, even when I remember how it used to be with Hailey, I barely feel anything. When I do jerk off it's mechanical and depressing, and sometimes I can't even finish. But with Fernanda, it's different, and after each night that I spend with her, I lie in bed and rethink every detail, each small touch.

"I'm sure he'll turn up," I say, and she frowns and puts her face into my neck, sighing. In the cracked street I can see three small children in plastic masks cowering behind the fence. Every so often one of them ventures a few yards out onto the dock, then runs back to join the others. The masks are bright red and bright yellow, too big for their faces, and they wobble a bit as the children run, the large sinister smiles and huge sagging eyes shaking.

They look like tiny demons as they dance. It's very unsettling. Yet I can't take my eyes off them.

Fernanda stares too, following my eyes. "I don't," she says, but I'm not sure if she means that she thinks that her brother is lost, or if she doesn't understand what I'm saying. It doesn't matter. We stare out at the flat sun, setting so low and close it feels like we could reach out and touch it. The waves that moved so restlessly before have disappeared, and two fishing boats steer smoothly toward us, the voices of the men echoing. Fernanda seems more frantic today, her hands jabbing into my back as we kiss, squeezing the back of my neck, sliding under my shirt to rake through the hair on my chest.

"Come," Fernanda says finally, untangling herself and standing.

"Where?"

She nods and holds out her hand to me, motioning for me to stand. She does that a lot—gestures to me instead of talking. I guess she's embarrassed by her poor English, either that or she's annoyed by the fact that I get confused so easily. I wonder if she knows that I've been good and drunk every time we've been together. The last time we were together, her teeth and lips became stained with red from the icy daiquiris I bought for her.

We walk quickly through streets where rusty cars and motorbikes blow dust into the air. When we stop at a crosswalk, I pull her to me and we kiss. My hands fall below her waist but she yanks them back up. My heart pounds and I am sweaty and dizzy and drunk and I want her so badly suddenly that wild thoughts fly through my head, of marrying Fernanda, of settling here with her, by the ocean.

"Where are you taking me?" I whisper.

She doesn't answer, just points to the cross that hangs around her neck and smiles. I reach out and touch the cold metal, then press my palm against the soft skin of her chest.

"Come," she says again, "soon, there."

We cut through someone's yard, and then before us is the *catedral*, a giant silver cone that pokes through the darkening clouds. Fernanda and I stand outside, surrounded by a small crowd of people who appear to be comforting each other. A pack of stray dogs runs by, patchy fur sucked to the bones of their ribs. The larger dogs chase the smallest, who lets out a high-pitched whine. I know that tonight they'll turn on him, eat him just to survive. I've seen it happen.

Fernanda takes my hand again and leads me inside, where the carpets are red and the walls are stone, decorated with gold. I've never been in here before, only passed by once or twice. The walls slope together and come to a point far above us in the musty darkness. We pass a short priest with a shiny forehead, whose white robe drags the floor, and he nods and whispers something. The smell of incense hangs over the empty pews.

We sit down together in the corner against the wall. I want to ask what we're doing, but I'm not sure what to say or how to say it. There are only three other people here. There is no Mass being said. But after a few minutes Fernanda looks up expectedly and then motions for me to stand.

"My family come pray for Marcello come back. *Minha irmão.* Everyone look for him."

I didn't know that was his name. I'm wondering if we can get a drink somewhere after this. We move down as a group of people slides slowly into our pew and eases onto their knees. "Your dad?" I ask. "Your mom?"

Fernanda hesitates, looking down the row at the faces of her relatives. "No," she says, "no here." She gestures toward the door. "Out, out. They out."

She motions for me to kneel alongside her, and she takes my hand and closes her eyes. Her eyelids are trembling ever so slightly. She grips my hand so tightly that it hurts.

I close my eyes, too, and my head spins in the blankness. I haven't thought of my other life, I haven't thought of Before, all night. Maybe there is still time for me. Maybe I can stay here, work, marry Fernanda, and just *live.* I could even come to church. Maybe it wasn't a question of forgetting, but of replacing things.

I open my eyes because there is some commotion near the doorway. I hear muffled words being exchanged, and then the room fills with shuffling and banging as everyone rises. The priest is standing beside the door with a woman, and I vaguely recognize her. She has short black hair—was she on the beach earlier? The priest embraces her, makes the sign of the cross, and somberly announces something. There is an immediate buzz of anxious chatter and gasps.

"*Mãe,*" Fernanda whispers, her voice catching in her throat.

"What?" I ask, but she doesn't seem to hear me. "What'd he say?"

But everyone is filing out nervously, pushing against each other as if the room is on fire. Fernanda rips her hand away from mine, and as I try to grab her she breaks for the doorway, weaving through the crowd, sobbing.

I want to run after her, to comfort her. But I sit back down.

Everyone has gone outside, and the priest has disappeared behind the altar. Shadows flicker on the walls, and Jesus is pinned up all over the place, dying a hundred different deaths. He's dying behind the altar, staring at me out of a statue the color of stone, and as I tilt my neck back to look up, Jesus is suffering on each sloping stone wall, drawn crudely in what looks like black crayon. I reach my free hand out to touch the drawing, but when I take it away from the cold stone, there's nothing there. No blood, no crayon, nothing. I stare at Jesus and he stares back at me, mute, unable to do anything to help me.

I clamber outside, dizzy, trying to regain my balance. The priest places a hand on my back as I walk out—he's mistaken my drunkenness and confusion for sorrow. The sky has grown dark. When it rains in the tropics of Brazil, there is no warning, and no escape. Suddenly the droplets, as big as quarters, hammer your head and sting your bare arms. I wrap my arms around myself and scan the street for Fernanda, but there are people swarming everywhere now. The dark street hisses at me as the rain begins.

Suddenly a truck pulls up to the curb, its tires screeching, and the woman with the black hair breaks from the crowd and rushes toward it. She's dragging Fernanda behind her. I open my mouth to call out to her but find I can't.

The rain bounces off the cobblestones angrily. The driver's side of the car opens, and a man wearing only a pair of wet shorts gets out and opens the back door. Another man from the crowd joins him, and together they reach into the backseat and slowly pull out a body.

"Marcello!" Fernanda screams, but her voice is drowned out by the rain. More shrieks follow as the crowd throngs toward the slumping head, the skinny legs that jut limply from cut-off shorts. Fernanda's eyes turn, aflame, searching the crowd, and I step back into the doorway of the church, bumping into someone who shoves me away. Fernanda's mother now, too, looks out into the crowd as she holds up the head of her son, her face white, crying out rapidly in Portuguese. I can't hear her with the rain and the wind, but I wouldn't be able to understand her anyway. Fernanda is screaming hysterically, her hand on the boy's cheek.

I turn into the empty church. The priest has vanished. My clothes are soaked and dripping. Foreign voices echo in the street outside and sting my ears. The air smells of incense and wood, and I duck into the last pew and close my eyes.

At some point, I feel Emily come. She slumps next to me, her head on my shoulder. I thankfully reach out and put my arm around her, pull her close. But even in my haze I know something isn't right. She's much too big. This can't be my daughter. I keep my eyes closed, but a heavy pressure grips my chest.

It's Hailey. She presses her mouth against my neck, her nose cold, and breathes in haltingly, remembering how I smell. I reach out and wrap my hands around hers. I'm wet and cold but she nestles against me, begging my body to warm hers. I'm surprised only by how good this feels, at how tightly we press against each other.

Our shivering is the only sound in the church. Hailey murmurs something dreamily into my shoulder about how nice it is to finally be here. About waiting for Emily to get there and how excited she is to see her and go home afterward, all of us together. I can see the three of us walking out of the church into the yellow glow of the streetlights. The rain will have stopped. The crowd will be gone.

Hailey shifts position, wrapping my arm around her and pressing her back against me, drifting off. Her hair is covering my face but I don't want to move. I don't know how long we sit there. I feel my clothes begin to dry and stiffen. My legs begin to ache. Footsteps echo and fade. At some point Hailey awakens. She whispers that she is almost ready to leave, and her breath is warm against my cheek.

"But where is she?" she asks, sounding puzzled. Her voice is muffled against my sleeve. "Scott?"

And with that, the sharp, throbbing pain in my head returns, and I open my eyes. Blood pounds in my temples, cold sweat drips down my back and mixes with the rain. Fernanda is leaning on my shoulder. She looks up at me, her eyes wide. Her hands are warmer than mine, and she gently touches the tips of my thumbs, and then presses her fingers against my wrist, as if checking for a pulse.

teach me

This could be the week that the money would run out. Catarina knew that she had to be conscious of that possibility. As she walked down Cuesta de Gomérez toward Placeta de la Miga, the air shimmered, a foggy curtain in the blazing heat. Her heels felt uneven, and it was hard not to trip on the cobblestones. The hills behind her that held la Alhambra, with its palaces and gardens and trickling water, whispered mockingly. In the tourism magazine she'd found in her hotel room, Catarina had read that this was the last Muslim city to fall to the Christians, at the hands of Queen Isabel of Castilla and her husband, Ferdinand II of Aragon. Their bodies were still buried there. Catarina loved the sound of the queen's name, *Isabel de Castilla*. She wondered how many people had died up there, and if Isabel herself had done any of the killing.

A taxi slowed next to her, and the driver gestured and honked. Catarina shook her head. The owner of the hotel, staring at her across the front desk this morning, had insisted that she take a cab. When she refused, he had squeezed his hands together tightly and peered at her curiously.

"I'd rather walk," she'd told him, staring directly at the thick, streaky lenses of his glasses. Finally, he wrote out directions for her, shaking his head. Take a bus at least, he'd muttered, repeatedly circling the bus station on the map until it looked as thought the point of his pencil would snap. Catarina understood only part of what he said. When she'd arrived three days before, he'd glared hungrily at her as she checked in, and then made sure he informed her that he was the *owner* of the hotel and did not merely work there. The last remnants of his thinning hair were carefully combed and plastered to his head, and Catarina immediately knew that she would be able to stay in the hotel for free, if it came to that. She hoped it wouldn't, but it was good to know.

This morning he'd hurriedly explained that to have a bullfight of this caliber in Granada was *especial, muy especial,* and that she was *muy afortunado* to be there for it. Tickets would be hard to come by—she'd better get there early. The bullfighter, whose name was José Blanco, was *especial, fantástico, el mejor,* and he might not come around here again. Maybe Madrid, or Barcelona. But not here.

"Oh, maybe I'll follow him," Catarina said, smiling, and the man blinked and then laughed hesitantly, showing small yellow teeth.

Another taxi slowed down next to her. For a moment she longed to fold herself into the backseat. Instead, she pushed on toward the stadium. She had to begin to be more economical, she scolded herself. She had to take a step down from the comfortable hotels she'd been staying in. El Hotel Puerta de las Granadas was far too luxurious for her.

Catarina passed a small bar where workers were breaking for lunch at an outdoor table. They watched her pass, the thin cotton dress she'd bought a few days ago sticking to her where she was already sweating, her pocketbook strap pinned across her chest. She rolled her eyes and sighed, pouted so they could see. She didn't want a man, necessarily. But she needed money. She'd been frugal with the cash she had stolen—she still had some American dollars, even—the rest she'd changed into Euros. Max had cancelled one of the credit cards; she hadn't known until she tried to book a hotel room and was denied. Strangely, he'd left the other credit line open. A parting gift? A gesture he thought might bring her back? Catarina grimaced at the thought of him reading the statements online, pursing his lips as he imagined what she was up to. Keeping tabs on her. Well, for now, she needed his money. It was unavoidable. She'd even called the bank the other day from the hotel and tried to extend the credit limit of eight thousand dollars, but they'd told her she wasn't authorized. She still had about six thousand to spare, but she'd been planning on going to a bank and trying for a cash advance. That way, if Max grew fed up and terminated the account, she'd be able to go on. Somehow, though, the idea of running out of money didn't frighten her the way she thought it would. She'd go on. She knew she would. It had become that simple.

The walk was longer than she thought, though, and she was beginning to cave. She hadn't eaten anything, just gulped some warm juice in the lobby, and her mouth was dry and chalky. She checked the map—this was Calle Cuesta de Escoriaza. She hadn't made it very far. There was a small café across the street, and when she walked in, all that greeted her were a few dusty tables and a white counter with stools. Catarina ordered iced water, a beer, and a meat empanada. She finished half of the beer quickly, drank some of the water, and then was served the pastry on a small white plate. When she'd finished everything, she stood up and paid the woman at the counter, who looked at her blankly and said nothing.

Catarina followed the directions, walking on crumbling sidewalks through traffic circles and onto main avenues where small, rusted cars buzzed by. Some honked at her. She waited in the shade for the bus, fingering the folded bills, counting them in her head. Droplets of sweat trickled down, and the skin over her ribs itched. Next to her, two Muslim women leaned against each other, draped in heavy robes. All Catarina could see were their eyes, which followed her as she clandestinely sniffed herself. She'd forgotten to put on deodorant, or it had melted away.

The driver, an old man wearing a wilted white cap, nodded to her when she got on. She slid into a seat and closed her eyes. Behind her, the womens' voices rippled and jerked in the breeze. Catarina worked up some spit and swallowed. She'd have more cold beer when she got there.

Outside the Plaza de Toros, people milled about, kicking up dry dust. She wandered until she found a ticket window and eventually purchased one ticket from a grinning young girl with braided hair and braces. When she wiped her face with a white napkin, it came away covered in brown dirt.

Beer was served in large plastic cups. Catarina bought two. She climbed rows of stone steps behind older couples who took the steps one at a time, men with children on their shoulders, and young boys running and tripping in anxious groups. When she finally sat down and breathed in, she felt dizzy. Down in the ring, the carefully raked brown dirt reminded her of the manicured fields of Max's favorite sport—the baseball games he'd sit for hours in front of, alternately yelling and dozing off. In the corners of the ring, horses stamped their feet and men hurriedly jogged about. The open seats were filling up now. To her left, a family that smiled at her, with two little boys who stretched and climbed everywhere, even onto her lap. To her right, a somber, elderly man with a white hat and a neatly trimmed gray beard, holding a bottle of wine that he uncorked and took a long pull from.

"Rioja," he said, offering it to her. Everyone assumed she was Spanish—before she spoke, at least. The wine was warm and dry, and it caught in her throat. The man patted her wet back.

It began. Catarina could hear the whispers of the small boys sparking like wooden matches. Transfixed, the children stopped moving, their mouths open. *José . . . Señor Blanco . . . José . . .* his name twitched on everyone's lips. Every woman's eyes set on his slim shoulders. He was cloaked in shining black, the colored sequins on his back winking in the afternoon sun. He jogged out to the center of the ring, waved to the four sides of the stadium, and then disappeared. Catarina had finished the first cup of beer, and she let the other one rest against her, already lukewarm. Again, there was that urge to close her eyes. She was here—the seat digging into the backs of her legs, the musty smell of body odors mixing—and she was anywhere. Max was back in the States, in what was becoming another world. Shannon and Walter too. But maybe she'd never really belonged with them, she thought. Maybe she'd never really belonged in the States. Catarina sipped her beer and thought back to when she first got there, when she met Manny, whose restaurant she'd worked in, and then Helena. She'd been surprised by the joy that filled her when she heard Helena's voice in her backyard, speaking her language. It was so much more beautiful and intimate than the flat, clunky English that she'd struggled to learn. Catarina remembered Nuno, and how he used to watch her through the windows. Paulo, with his muscles and painfully tight grip, still going through the tired motions of his life back in Rhode Island, still married to that sad, worn woman whom he didn't love.

Maybe Catarina could find something here, something that had been missing in the States. It wasn't a house overlooking the water, or an endless drive down I-95, or the cool bite of a glass of *vinho verde* after a long night's work. It wasn't money, or sex, or love, or family—it was none of the things that people normally sought after. It was, maybe, something that she would know only when she saw it. Catarina sipped her beer and felt, for the first time in years, faint stirrings of hope in her chest. There was nothing in Portugal for her anymore, and now, nothing left in the States. But in between? In between, perhaps there was everything.

"*El mejor!*" croaked the man next to her, pressing the bottle against her arm. This time she drank evenly and didn't choke. Behind her, a pack of teenagers stamped their feet and clapped their hands, and she smelled the burnt, brown-sugar scent of hashish wafting down.

The first bull was led out on two ropes, both attached to its neck, and the crowd erupted in whistles and hisses as it was released in the center of the ring. Catarina watched it skulk about, black and heaving. It was slower than she had thought it would be, and she felt herself tense up as a man on horseback rapidly approached, wielding what looked like a barbed stick. His horse wore some sort of shiny armor. The bull had no hope of running, and when it tried to, the rider flew up alongside of him and plunged the stick into the back of his neck again and again, until black blood oozed from a hole there, and the bull heaved and twitched and stumbled.

Was this it, then? Was this the fight? Next to Catarina, the old man's eyes gleamed. He nodded to her. "*Ahora,*" he said, pointing.

So, *now* it was time. Catarina felt silly and stupid. She should have understood that it hadn't started yet.

José Blanco suddenly strutted out, his walk quick, purposeful. Catarina was blinded as the crowd rose, clapping, and the man next to her yanked her up so she could see. José was no longer wearing black, but a shiny red and gold outfit that sparkled in the sun. He held what looked like a sword.

He approached the bull as if it were a car he were getting into, or a plane he was about to board. When he was ten feet away, he brandished his red cape and bent down to his knees. The bull twitched and stamped its feet, leaning to one side. José Blanco inched closer, taunting him, waving the cape, and suddenly the animal snorted and charged, horns ripping at the air, red mouth snapping open. Just when it looked as though there was nowhere for the bullfighter to go, he sidestepped and twirled, and his knife flashed in the air, flicked sharp, and stuck.

"*Olé!*" The crowd responded on cue, and one of the children next to her slapped Catarina's arm. The bull spun in circles, the glittering knife wedged in his shoulders. The routine played itself out twice more, and after the third knife had been jerked into flesh with ease, the animal staggered and collapsed. Three white horses dragged his body away.

Catarina watched each bull intently, stopping only to order beer from the vendors who circled the stadium. Each animal was different, she decided, in the same way that people were. Each one reacted differently to the first attack. Some cowered, and others grew emboldened, snapping and writhing in the warm grip of pain.

Catarina followed each bull after it was dragged away, as most of the crowd turned back to their peanuts and beer, their arms tightening around wives or husbands, girlfriends or boyfriends. While José Blanco smiled and waved, in the corner of the ring a smaller man bent to his knees and twisted a short dagger into each bull's neck.

The shock began to wear off. It became routine, cyclic. The spray of blood on the dry dirt, the clouds of dust that stung her eyes, the slap of the bull's body on the ground. But Catarina had to agree with the man at the hotel; there was something about this bullfighter, this José Blanco. Anyone could see that. Even from high above, Catarina could see the sharpened features of his face, as if he'd been drawn with a pencil and ruler. A cropped black beard gripped his cheeks and chin tightly, and his body was both taut and malleable. Did he have bones, José Blanco? He moved differently than any man she had ever seen, almost like a dancer, almost, she thought, laughing, like a young girl trying to run from her own shadow. He edged so close to the third bull that he hung a piece of cloth from one of its horns, the animal spitting at him and pounding its hooves into the ground, but for some reason, not moving. José Blanco laughed, gestured to the crowd, and bowed deeply

"*Está loco!*" The man next to her extended his package of thin brown cigars, the next step in what seemed like his own routine. They were tightly wrapped, perhaps homemade. Catarina let him light one for her as he stared at her thighs.

But it was one of the last bulls that presented a problem. Rangy and thin, he snarled his way around the ring, and when the man on horseback came to incite him, he jerked his head and stabbed one of his horns into the horse's smooth white belly. The crowd gasped as the horse cracked its head back and shrieked, blood pouring from its stomach, and men from all directions rode in—some frantically distracting the bull, others leading the limping horse to safety.

The crowd leaned forward as José Blanco entered the ring calmly, almost delicately. When the sun hit his back and shoulders, he nearly disappeared in a burst of colored glitter and flame. He twirled and jabbed and slipped the first two swords in perfectly, the bull raging and tearing around the ring, easily the fastest animal so far. But on the third sword, the bull hooked José Blanco's armpit with his horn, the rip of clothing echoing up through the stands, the silver arm of his shirt plunging dark red. Silence rained over the crowd as José collapsed in a cloud of dust. Men on horseback charged into the ring to save him, the pounding of hooves like drums, keeping the bull away from José with vicious swings of their swords. Catarina blinked her eyes to try to rid them of the dust. *Wait, is this normal?* she wanted to ask the hushed stadium, the mothers who covered their children's eyes.

But with the bull distracted, José Blanco leapt up, ran, and drove the knife into the bull's back before limping out of the ring, one arm raised in victory. The crowd broke into stunned applause.

"*Llévalo al hospital!*" shouted the man next to her.

"Will he come back?" asked Catarina. "Come back? Return?"

"*No lo sé,*" he said in disbelief, his eyes large and reddened. He took off his hat and solemnly placed it over his heart. "*José Blanco, él es el mejor,*" he said somberly, crossing himself.

Catarina's mind seesawed back and forth, greased by the beer and wine. When the first bull fell, she had felt a sense of satisfaction, of relief. But as the hours passed, she found that she deeply hated all of it—the dark blood that fell freely to the dirt, the hoarse, hungry cries of the crowd, even José Blanco with his shiny clothes and rubbery limbs. She wanted the bull to win, to escape, to have some kind of chance in all of this. All around her, old people were living out their last days, knowing their hour was coming, while young children, like the boys squirming next to her, remained blissful in their ignorance. Which was better? What did her mother used to say affectionately, long ago, about Catarina's father when he left home to travel? *A sorte protege os audazes.* Luck protects the daring ones. And she supposed there was a chance that luck had protected him for a long time, though she wasn't sure from what. Catarina wanted to believe that luck had protected Queen Isabel of Castilla, too, as she wielded her sword, fighting to overtake a new kingdom with blood smeared on her long fingers.

She'd been daring lately, hadn't she? But would her mother be proud of her, or angry that she left Sintra to drift aimlessly around the States? To settle in New England and then pick up and leave again, before she could feel any roots start to grow? Catarina knew that her mother would have no right to be upset with anyone but herself, for leaving her family when Catarina was young. For showing her daughter that it was fine to just pick up and run before you were trapped forever. Catarina wasn't stupid—she was aware of the connection between their behaviors. But she never felt as though her decisions were inspired by what her mother had done, and if anyone suggested that, she'd scoff at them. *Isso é absurdo,* she'd hiss through the slight gap between her two front teeth. She was her own person, and if people didn't understand that, then they didn't understand her.

But that's part of what she'd learned lately: the reasons behind things were meaningless. Origins. Impressions. It didn't matter what Max, or the man next to her, whose glazed eyes were beginning to burn into her skin, or anyone thought of her. Her father was dead, buried in Sintra, where the sun rose relentlessly each day over Praia de Adraga. Here, in Granada, there was the blazing heat of the afternoon and the heavy scent of blood in the air. And in this moment, as everyone around her delighted in the slaughter, Catarina found herself praying that José Blanco would himself be gored in the stomach by one of the bull's sharp white horns. No one had the right to own the world, as he seemed to. *C'mon,* she muttered to herself. *Get him. Get him.*

With each chance that José Blanco took, with each narrow escape from death, she felt what could only be described as a boiling in the pit of her stomach as strange, white-hot chills traced down her back. *Get him. Knock him down.* But it wasn't going to happen, and she knew that. The hero wasn't one of them. He was separate from all of this, and would remain untouched. He was separate from her, and her mother. There was nothing heroic about either of them; Catarina knew that.

And when José Blanco killed the last bull, quickly and efficiently, with less fanfare and ease but more cunning and force, driving the knife into the animal's back, Catarina felt herself, against her will, cheering. It was addicting—following his sharp movements, drinking as the shadows crept across the ring—she had to admit it. This was how it had always been, hadn't it? This is how it would always be. The sun beginning to fade, trails of smoke from cigarettes and cigars sifting down through the stands. The bull lying there in its massive black bulk, its eyes staring vacantly upward at the thousands gathered to watch it die.

Catarina knew the bull was questioning everything. Looking for answers. She shook her head. It wasn't worth it, she wanted to tell him. Just take what's coming to you.

—

Catarina pushed herself through the dank, sweaty crowd and ducked into the first place that she saw. The bartender placed a plate of olives and cheese in front of her, and she ate ravenously, spitting the pits into her hand and curling them into her napkin. She hadn't realized how thick the crowd would be on the street, and she was glad she'd escaped the hooting and hollering, the need to press her body through tight spaces.

But the silence lasted for only a few minutes. People began to pour in, their clothes dusty, their skin flushed. Catarina turned back to the bar and ordered another beer. She had not drunk this much beer before coming to Spain, but she'd begun to crave its bitter, icy coldness. When she awoke in her hotel room in the mornings, in a bed that was far too big for her, she would count down the hours to the time when she could have one.

Now there were elbows jabbing on each side of her, loud voices and singing, the yelling of names and clinking of glasses. And everywhere, the name José Blanco sung and whispered and toasted to. When the tapas plates were put down in front of her, they were grabbed by someone else's stained hands—there was no order to anything anymore. When the next plate came, she lunged, knocking over someone's wine glass, squeezing a handful of sliced ham and stuffing it into her mouth.

The bartender was watching her. Catarina wiped a greasy hand on her dress. When he turned away, she picked up a spoon and tried to see herself in the reflection, but it was impossible. Where was the bathroom? She ran a hand through her tangled hair and then crossed her arms and waited for the bartender to notice her. But when he turned back, his shirt clinging to his stocky frame, his eyes blazing, he was looking through her. And that's when she realized that the crowd, the chaos, had quieted. She spun around on her stool and watched through the glass as the line outside parted, men shoving each other, women's eyes lighting. The maître d' appeared suddenly, wearing a dark suit and running to open the heavy wooden door.

In between two taller men—bodyguards?—strode José Blanco. He was wearing a fitted dark suit, and his dark hair was still wet. His white collar leapt up from his shoulders, and his shoes caught the candlelight and glinted. His features were no softer than they'd appeared from high above—his nose was hawkish, his chin like the tip of a flat sword. But his eyes were wide open, the whites gleaming, his pupils seemingly as big as quarters. He took everything in: the crowd, the hushed silence, the cars that slowed to a crawl out in the street. A tiny line creased his forehead in surprise.

"Olé!" someone yelled, and then it was broken and the crowd split open into different cheers and songs, dancing and slapping hands together. A few stools down, a woman, in her zeal, slid off her seat and pitched to the ground. Next to her a man pounded the bar, trying for the bartender, begging only to buy a drink for José Blanco. But in that moment José was gone, ushered through the bar, his shoes clicking in time with the flash of cameras.

The crowd writhed anxiously. Where had he gone? Would he come back? Why did he come here, of all places? Catarina felt confidently above all of this. Who cared why he was here? He had come to the bar, and now he was gone. She thought he should have stayed out here, with the people, had a drink with his fans. She actually found it rude that he hadn't, and she would say it to his face if she had the chance.

But he had looked at her as he walked through. She was certain of it. Catarina played it back in her head, drank, played it again. Those enormous eyes had glided back and forth, back and forth, and then come to a stop in hers. He'd waited for her to recoil and look away. He'd probably expected her eyes to slip down to the bar, or her hands. But they hadn't. She had not smiled adoringly or teased her tongue over her lips. She had met his stare head-on, unblinking, and as he was rushed by her, he'd craned his neck to stay with her and stumbled very slightly. Then he was gone.

Rumors ignited. He knew the owner. He knew the bartender. He loved the *gambas al ajillo* here; it was his favorite.

No, no, argued the man next to her, and suddenly grabbed Catarina's arm. She didn't flinch. Her jaw locked, daring him.

"He's fucking a waitress," he said grimly in Spanish, nodding. "Trust me, I know."

Catarina shrugged. "How do you know?"

The man stared at her. "It's true," he said. "Okay?"

"Well, why should I believe you? Do you know her?"

The man glared at her. His lip rose to show his teeth.

Catarina pressed on. She couldn't help herself. "How do you know?" she asked sarcastically. "Hmm?"

The man looked at her. His eyes were set deeply in his face, and taut lines were strung under them. She could smell the garlic on his breath. "Maybe he is fucking you, too?" he laughed, his hand drifting lazily down, loosely brushing across her breasts.

"Or maybe he is fucking your wife," she said simply.

The blow knocked her off her chair and she fell sideways to the floor, her head glancing off the edge of the bar, then onto someone's feet. One of her legs was still angled upward, caught on the stool. She didn't move, but lay there perfectly still, the din of the crowd clanging high above her like a bell.

—

"It's fine, José," whispered Catarina.

José Blanco lay motionless beside her, his arms stretched wide. In the middle of his chest there was a dusting of black hair that trailed down his stomach in a tight line.

Catarina admired his naked body even as it betrayed him. This was only the second time this had happened, and they'd made love what seemed like hundreds of times. But she could tell that this cut him to the core, even as he tried to hide it. Just the fact that she knew, that she might sit in the stands one day and watch him kill for her, having seen him like this.

Everything in the room was still. She pulled the covers down, but the heat of the night kept pressing.

"I am not *done* yet, Catarina," he said finally, tucking his hands behind his head in one smooth motion. It seemed to her that everything he did had to be done quickly and quietly, or not at all. His nails were even and impeccably clipped. His clothes were ironed and creased with military precision. One morning, she saw him throw away an orange that he had not sliced evenly enough. She often awoke to the crisp clip of his knife on the wooden cutting board.

"Yes, you are." Catarina turned toward him but did not touch him. She felt the pressure of electricity in the thin space between them. "But there will be other chances for you."

At this his lips turned up in a thin smile, and his mustache quivered.

"How about right now?" he asked, reaching for her arm. She pulled away from his smooth dry fingers, the hands that so often held blades.

Each morning, after shaving, he clapped his hands once, magnificently, talcum powder exploding in a white cloud of smoke. Catarina often stood behind him and examined her newly hacked and dyed blonde hair in the mirror. It looked awful. She loved it. She had done it a few nights ago, sitting on the patio, with a Swiss Army knife that she had found on the floor of the bus on the way here. José had come out and sat behind her silently, watching.

"It's uneven," he had finally said, startling her. "It's quite uneven in the back, Catarina."

"Well, you could help, instead of just sitting there. And don't sneak up on me when I have a knife in my hand."

"A knife?" he scoffed. "That is not a knife."

"Come here," he said, pointing, and she reluctantly sat down in front of him on the floor. "Now, count how many sailboats you see out there." He gestured to the expanse of ocean that glittered in the afternoon sun.

"Here," she said, passing the red knife up to him.

He looked down with disgust. "I'll use my own."

His blade whistled tersely through the humid air. She got a sense that the messiness, the unevenness of the coiled strands, displeased him.

After he had gone inside, Catarina had stayed out on the patio, feeling the warmth of the sun on the back of her neck for the first time in years. Then she'd gone inside and spent an hour rubbing the dye into her dark hair, until, when she glanced at the mirror quickly, she didn't recognize herself. The next morning, all the clippings were gone. Catarina wondered if José had swept them up in the middle of the night, if he'd been unable to sleep because of the mess on the patio.

He reached for her, anxious to prove himself. She resisted but allowed him to run his hands along her thighs gently. "What does it feel like . . . to kill something? I want you to explain how it is for you."

He sighed and his hand dropped on his bare chest. "It is not something to be explained, my love."

"How did you learn?"

"I watched my father. He watched his father. This is how it goes."

He leaned on his elbow. "What do you want to do in the morning, Cat? Do you want to travel somewhere for a few nights? Take a train to Madrid? Have you been there?"

"I don't like to be called that," Catarina said flatly. She sighed and stared out the window into the darkness. She'd known José for only two weeks. When she remembered the night at the bar, it unnerved her that her memory came only in blurred flashes—that she couldn't differentiate between what she remembered and how José's story had filled in the blanks. She recalled with pride what she'd said to the man who hit her. When José had asked, she had told him, and he'd cocked his head, as if considering her. He approved, she thought, of her attitude, but maybe not her recklessness. She remembered coming to in the bar's back room, with its plush red couches. Someone holding a glass of water to her mouth, then a leaking cup of ice to her forehead. José had given orders sternly. He'd left her alone and then come back, flinging the door open, with the man who had hit her in tow. Behind him were the two bodyguards. The man shuffled in, overweight, sweating. He bowed his head.

"Is this him?" José had asked her. She nodded, tensing up. But that was all. He had nodded to the guards and the man was taken away, his head flopping back and forth, his mouth opening but nothing coming out. There were two things that José would not talk about. One was the injury he'd suffered that day in the ring—though she watched him methodically wrap his shoulder each night with gauze, never wincing, never blinking, a cigarette perched in his mouth—and the other was the man in the bar that night.

"I'd like to go somewhere, yes," Catarina said lazily. "But should I let you come with me?" Her fingertips lightly grazed his forehead, searching.

José snorted at this.

She placed her hand over his hand, on his chest, and then traced the red, curling line that the bull's horns had left. José steeled himself and did not flinch, did not move a muscle.

His eyes flickered over her body. She knew that he was waiting for her. He always seemed to be waiting for her when he was like this; in between fights with nothing to do. He left only to return with fresh bread, cheese, and fish. When he was gone, she sat on the patio against the wall, smoking and staring at the sea. When he came back, he seared the fish in a thick black pan while Catarina waited, listening to the hissing sound of the flesh burning. They ate it rare.

They had not asked anything of each other, not even their respective names, and only nodded when one of them felt the need to tell the other something. There had been few questions. Catarina did not know if this was because neither of them cared or neither of them wanted to know the answers.

"Do you get sick of it?" she asked. "Fighting them?"

"No," he said simply, and gently slid his arm around her waist, pulling so that she had no choice but to inch closer to him. "Because it is what I do."

Catarina closed her eyes and remembered how it felt to drive across the States, the open fields and cornstalks whipping by in Iowa, the dust of Arizona staining the sides of her pickup. She remembered the man she met in Utah, and the night they'd spent in his camper drinking silver cans of beer, how she'd found herself making love to him on the fake wood floor, sliding as it creaked. And that unmistakable feeling that had come as she was lying there after they'd finished. That no one knew where she was. That her life was completely hers and no one else's. But she'd felt guilty when she returned to her house in Rhode Island, and she'd decided that a normal American life was what she needed to make her feel whole. To complete things.

She'd been wrong. It hadn't worked. But that was over with. And she'd begun to think that if she stayed in Spain, maybe she could begin again, one last time.

Catarina reached for José's hand and felt the tense energy that gathered in his fingers. It was hot inside of the apartment. Even with the ocean breeze, the heat of the day seemed to collect and stick to her skin. Catarina was always sweating, but José's hands remained cool. He did not move as she touched the lines on his palm searchingly.

"Will you teach me?" Catarina asked again, digging her nails into his palm.

José Blanco hesitated, then nodded. He did not appear to feel pain. Her teeth in his shoulder, the tiny crescents of her fingernails branded into his back. Nothing.

"Then teach me how to lie," she said, closing her eyes, smiling and pressing down on his palm. "Teach me how to kill."

He leaned on his elbow, staring at her. His free hand traced the faint bruise that remained under her eye. It had gone from red and black to a deep blue, and now bore the faint, greenish-yellow hue of rot and decay.

"Not things that can be taught," he repeated softly, his fingers tracing down the middle of her neck.

Catarina smiled to herself as she watched his eyes begin to change. Each night, José slept on his back with the covers over his face, his hot breath hanging over him in such a way that if she touched his face, it would be warmer than the rest of his body. In the mornings, she watched him twitch under the covers for those few seconds when he was still cloaked in dreaming, the look on his face serene and innocent. He was different in some ways, yes, but he was also the same as all of them. Paulo, Max, Walter, the owner of the hotel who had looked so disconsolate when she checked out, even the man at the bar who struck her to the ground.

Catarina gripped José's hand with both of hers and thrust it between her legs. She wanted a bead of sweat to appear on his forehead. She wanted to see a flicker of doubt. But his face was as still and as dry as stone.

"Do you love me?" Catarina asked

He did not move his hand. He stared at the ceiling without blinking. The moment stretched and burned.

And then, Catarina watched his upper lip tremble ever so slightly, just for a second.

As she climbed on top of him, Catarina knew this was the last time. José Blanco tightened his grip around her waist. He closed his eyes and his movements quickened.

But it was too late. Catarina moved rhythmically, slowing him down, smiling to herself. Outside in the streets of Granada, sirens rang out. Brakes squealed.

away from the mountains and toward the sea

NUNO · 2000

Nuno sat inside the darkened bar at the Lusitania Club with the other men, who were mostly like himself, elderly and retired. On the television screen above them, players shoved and ran in bright uniforms across grass that kicked up behind them. Sometimes they fell to the ground, crying out as the crowd rose up in disbelief. Sometimes, Nuno could feel himself rising up, too, his vision becoming sharper, clearer, as he drifted into the old world on the small screen. Up from the locker room in Estádio José Alvalade, his boots clicking and clacking across the cement, and then onto the field where he played as he used to, feinting and sliding and forgetting everything else.

But most days, Nuno's eyes watered and blurred, and the fantasy didn't work right. The games were getting harder to follow, he had to keep sitting closer to the TV. He drank his wine and nodded, muttering names to himself, absently rubbing the tiny scar on his bottom lip. At halftime he stood slowly and walked outside. It was November in Narragansett, and he blinked as the cold wind blew right through him. The air smelled of brine, and chimney smoke from the houses nearby.

Halftime was fine. It meant there was another forty-five minutes of football, and anything could happen. Sporting, down 1–0, could come back. It was after the game that the thinking started, during the drive home to the small house where he now lived alone since his wife, Helena, had died three months earlier. He pictured his breakfast dishes neatly stacked in the sink, the unblinking answering machine that his son, Paulo, had brought over for Christmas years ago. Helena had always hated the way it beeped incessantly to signal a message, and often Nuno had returned home to find that in desperation the plug had been yanked out of the wall.

Maybe today he would do something different. Stay at the club for a while after the game, play cards, smoke a cigar. Maybe there would be some English Premier League on or some highlights that he hadn't seen yet.

But he knew this was wishful thinking. He couldn't stay, not anymore.

Sporting Lisbon tied the game in the sixty-first minute. Many men clapped, but some refrained, shaking their heads as if any gloating could jinx it.

The game ended in a tie, and afterward, Luis, the bartender, came over and pointed to Nuno's empty glass. Nuno shook his head.

"Good game, huh?" Luis placed the glass in the sink and leaned back on the bar. Nuno noticed the wrinkles that lined his forehead and how his hair had grown entirely white. It was strange to think that he and Luis were both widowers now.

"Ah, they should've won," Nuno said quickly, shaking his head in disgust.

"Hey, Paulo was in here the other day, did he tell you?"

"What day?"

"Wednesday, I think?"

"For what?"

"He came in, watched a few games, had some drinks. A lot of drinks, actually. Said it was his midweek break." Luis grinned. "He's too much, always busting balls."

"He just drinks too much," Nuno scoffed. He wondered why Paulo hadn't called to invite him, or stopped by. What had Nuno done on Wednesday? Watched TV, cooked dinner. Or was that Tuesday? It didn't matter. His son should've called him.

Luis slapped his hand on the bar and fiddled with the TV remote, mumbling to himself, and Nuno thanked him, slid off his stool, and headed for the door.

On the way home he realized he was driving too quickly. He checked the time and tried to slow down. But there was something inside of him, welling up, and he pressed the accelerator again and shifted in his seat.

Catarina. She was usually home by now, walking through the yard as she always did, then going in. To change her clothes. Nuno turned down his street and coasted to a stop, breathing deeply.

Her rusty Chevy pickup wasn't there yet. He took the mail from the box as he went in, barely looking at it. Inside he used the bathroom quickly and then peeked out again over the sink, waiting for her to pull in. He could do nothing else. He felt a little tremor run through him—her soft brown skin, her thin dresses, the first time he saw her breasts in the pale white of daylight—and he shivered.

The best window to start from was over the sink. That was where he had been standing when he had first seen her on that Saturday afternoon, months ago. He had been doing the dishes when she cut across his yard, heading toward the small house behind his that she had just begun renting. It was a squat shack, on top of which sat a rickety upstairs extension framed with windows. The shingles were peeling away, the paint flaking off; the place had been ignored for years by the neighborhood.

Today it was four-thirty and growing dark when the faded red truck coughed and shuddered off in her driveway. Nuno watched, riveted, as she slid down from her seat, stretched, and walked to her mailbox. Nothing there. Her feet rustled the dry leaves as she walked across the yard.

As she entered the house, Nuno followed her through different windows, hunching down to look at her through the cracks he left between the windowsills and the blinds. Today she wore blue jeans and a white T-shirt, and her long black hair was wound in two tight tails that swung against her back.

When the door latch clicked and she went inside, he immediately went upstairs, as was the routine. He kept all of the blinds raised just a few inches. To keep it cool, he told himself when he felt strange about it, usually in the morning when he woke, chiding himself on this new habit, ashamed of the way that he kept chairs at each window to make it easier on his back.

She, on the other hand, never closed the blinds. He didn't think there *were* any blinds. The house was unfurnished, unfinished really. He had been in there once, years before, to help move someone in, or out. He wasn't sure, couldn't remember. Still, more than once Nuno wondered if she had any idea what he was doing. It was just too easy, wasn't it? The way his bedroom windows looked slightly down into hers, the way everything lined up. It was impossible to resist, even when he tried. Sometimes Nuno caught only glimpses of her and stared hungrily at an arm, a bare leg. The tattoo that he was startled to see one day wrapped around the small of her back. But glimpses were enough.

She turned on the radio, he could hear it faintly, and then disappeared for a while. He couldn't find her anywhere, even when he tried the small window in the bathroom, walking in circles, frustrated. Nuno passed pictures of Paulo, Helena, and himself throughout the house, and he was thankful for their silence. He avoided all of them, especially the old black-and-white of Helena and him at the airport in Lisbon. It was taken by a stranger on the day that they left Portugal. Nuno used to stop and admire his square jawline, his thick black mustache. Now, if he glanced at it, he only wondered what his young self would do if he saw him criss-crossing the house, hunched over, following Catarina. And he couldn't bring himself to even look at Helena—her tight-lipped smile, the way she glared unnervingly at the camera. He had been nervous that day, he remembered, double-checking their passports, ushering them quickly through the lines. She had stayed silent and moved on her own terms, smiling at the clusters of people as if the chaos appealed to her.

Suddenly, through the biggest window in his bedroom, Catarina reappeared. Nuno saw the flash of movement out of the corner of his eye, made it to the window as fast as he could, and then perched on the edge of a chair, sweating.

Her jeans were gone, replaced by white underwear; her T-shirt hung to the tops of her thighs. She was folding something, bending down, singing with the music, tapping her foot. Nuno clenched his hands into fists and wouldn't blink, instead trying to freeze the image like a photograph. The phone rang, she disappeared, and then seconds later appeared again, *her shirt gone*—he breathed in sharply as she rummaged through drawers, her body fluid and soft and whiter in places. His eyes watered, and the chalky heat caught in the back of his throat.

She disappeared and he thought he heard her running through the house, banging down the stairs. Then came the creak and slam of the door, the car rustling and cracking, started, gone.

He leaned weakly against the window, his feet suddenly sore, and let his warm forehead touch the cool glass.

—

Catarina had moved in six months ago. Nuno had watched her only once during that time, through the bathroom window, spreading the blinds with shaking fingers, surges of guilt and surprise running like chills up his back until Helena called for him to come and eat. He dropped the blinds with a snap and made himself promise never to do it again, watching the lines on his face move in the mirror as he spoke. A few days later Helena had asked him if he'd met the new neighbor yet.

"She's *bonita*," she said as they ate dinner, "but alone, Nuno, *jovem e sozinha!*" she exclaimed, plucking the serving spoon from the bowl of rice and waving it at him. She went on and on until Nuno grew tired of it and left her busy with the dishes.

He didn't want to meet her, didn't even want to know her name. When he saw her outside, he forced himself to look away, waving to her briskly just so he would not seem impolite. He knew Helena spent time with her during the day when he was at the club, but Catarina was always gone when he returned, for which he was thankful.

Helena had died on August sixth. Nuno came home to find her sitting at the kitchen table with her head down. After he checked her wrist for a pulse and listened for her heartbeat, he called 9-1-1 and sat next to her at the table, sweating. When the ambulance came, he barely spoke to the young men who took her away, telling them only that he would meet them at the hospital later and that he did not wish to ride with them.

It was not how he had thought it would be, finding her there. They had been married fifty years before, in Lagos, at the Igreja de Santa Maria, under the shining statue of Jesus and facing away from the mountains and toward the sea, as was the custom. When he found her, it was not how he had imagined it at all. Because his first thought, before his chest ached and his throat closed, before the phone calls and flowers that smelled of mildew filled the kitchen, before learning to sleep without feeling her breath on his wrinkled cheek, his first thought was that he could watch Catarina every day now. It didn't matter anymore. It just didn't matter.

In the weeks and months that followed, he spent even more time at the club, joining the other retired men at the bar, watching football. Paulo and sometimes his wife, Claire—whom Nuno had always found sweet but lifeless, very unlike a *Portuguesa*—came to visit him fairly often. But it surprised him how quickly he grew accustomed to living alone.

Eating supper in front of the television each night, he often remembered how the neighborhood used to be when they first arrived, all of them Portuguese, fresh. Gathering on Sundays at East Matunuck Beach, hundreds of them maybe, the rich, salty smell of *caldeirada* in giant bowls, the *sardinhas assadas* beside loaves of coarse bread, the murky water full of purple seaweed. Watching Paolo swim and wrestle in the water with the other boys as it grew dark. Now they had all drifted away from the old places, the South County beaches and backyards with bocce and horseshoes and even the Lusitania Club. It wasn't the way it used to be, anymore.

But Catarina. Walking by the windows, her body so languid, her skin seemingly so smooth to the touch. When he took out the garbage at night, Nuno could smell the onions and olives that she used in her *bacalhau*, and when he had woken hard the other morning, thinking of her, he lay there groggy and surprised, almost afraid to move. It hadn't happened in years, but he didn't think it had anything to do with Helena. He was seventy-five, he told himself. His body had stopped working like that years before. He didn't desire anyone, even the nude women he saw sometimes on cable television. A beautiful woman now was like a painting; his eyes wrapped around the curves and shine, but he felt and wanted nothing.

But maybe he had been wrong. Now Nuno watched Catarina anytime that he could, staring greedily and waiting for the warmth to rise in the base of his stomach and spread downward. He began paying attention to when she came home at night. He wondered what she did to be out so late.

He strained to stay awake, watching the local news, Red Sox highlights, and taped football matches on RTP and Univision. Late at night, leaning back in his leather recliner, waiting for her, his life sometimes rewound a bit in the darkness and blue flickering.

About three times a week, just as he had been doing for years, Nuno went to his grandson's football matches. Paulo had never been very good, Nuno admitted, but his son, Scott, was becoming one of the state's best soccer players.

Nuno had grown up playing on club teams in Lagos. He had been a fierce, temperamental defender, and there was constantly a cautionary yellow card being raised over his head. During a recent game, Nuno had told Paulo that Scott should try to go to Portugal and play; there was more opportunity there for young players. Paulo shook his head and snorted.

"Nope, he'll go to college, Dad," he said sharply, his eyes darting to follow the action. Suddenly Scott raced for the ball and was tripped. As he lay on the ground, entangled with one of the defenders, they could see the pushing and punching and watched as the defender jabbed Scott in the stomach with his elbow. Whistles echoed in the cool air.

Paulo stormed through the crowd and down the metal bleachers, his face strangely white, the veins in his temples bulging. On his way he knocked into another player's mother and she pitched forward and cried out, but he didn't stop until he reached the sideline, where he screamed and flapped his arms. The referee ran over, looked once into Paulo's eyes, and ordered him to leave the grounds before he called the police.

They sat in the car with the heat hissing at them and watched the rest of the game. "If Scott is hurt because of this, I will find that kid," Paulo said, his jaw locked. "Right, Dad?" But Nuno just stared through the dirty windshield at the field.

"What's wrong with you?" he said finally, slapping his son roughly on the arm. "Why—why would you—"

"You would have done the same fucking thing if it was me out there," snapped Paulo. "Don't even start."

Nuno left the car then, walking across the parking lot where the shadows mixed with damp leaves. He would greet Scott when he came off the field, congratulate him on a well-played game, and then bring him to see his father.

⌒

It was the last Friday in November, and Sporting Lisbon was poised to defeat the Italian team Juventus in the first round of the Champions League. At the club, as the wine was poured and raised and poured again, Nuno almost told. He stood outside as Luis smoked a cigarette, and they watched a pack of girls from the high school stride by in short skirts, giggling, their faces painted with makeup. Luis raised his eyebrows and winked, but Nuno shook his head and scowled. Because it wasn't like that. Catarina was different, older. She was put there for him. He told himself that she was from Lagos, not Sintra, where he'd heard the other men say she was from. She was from the small town where he was born, where cobblestone streets, white houses with rust-red roofs, and palm trees led to the ocean.

That night in bed he found himself thinking of Helena, of when they met. He was sixteen and she was eighteen, and they used to make love on the beach, him pushing into her as she sank under him. Afterward in the warm water, he floated on his back, spinning small circles with his hands. Helena floundered and splashed in the white light of the moon, kicking at the surface as if trying to tame it. But you needed to lie quiet and still and let the salt and the water hold you, and he'd never been able to teach her.

When he married her in Lagos, it was because he believed it was what they both wanted, and needed. They'd grown up in the same small town and found themselves drawn together. Like many lovers, they'd had their problems, but Nuno didn't really allow himself to think about those things much anymore. It only messed things up, he thought, thinking about what he'd done wrong as a kid. It was too hard, and he was too old to deal with it.

He remembered, though, that when he told Helena that he'd arranged for them to move to the States, she'd grown furious, screaming and cursing at him for not telling her of his plans, surprising him. Nuno explained that it was the only way he could provide for them, but she didn't want to hear it, and swore she wouldn't leave her parents. Helena wouldn't speak to him for a week, and Nuno remembered the straight red line of her lips, the thick silences that slid in between them like heavy panes of glass. Finally, after weeks of her family urging her to go, Helena agreed, and her lips broke into a smile. They would move together, she said, and be happy. That was it. But there was a part of Nuno that wondered where all of her biting anger had gone.

On Sunday Paulo surprised him, coming over earlier than usual. Nuno was upstairs in his bedroom, watching Catarina hang clothes on the line in the haze of the setting sun. She was wearing a long skirt that rippled around her legs in the wind. When Catarina went inside, Nuno sat on the bed, unbuttoned his pants, and followed her silhouette from room to room, breathing heavily. But suddenly he heard his son's voice echoing through the house.

"Dad?"

Nuno fell sideways onto the bed and just lay there, fumbling, heaving, buttoning up right before Paulo burst in.

"Dad? What are you doing, taking a nap?

Nuno raised himself and wiped his face with his hands. "I was—"

"I thought we were going for dinner? You okay?"

"I'm fine. I guess I forgot. Didn't hear you come in."

Nuno escaped into the hallway. He could hear Paulo yanking up all the shades.

"So fucking dark in here," he said. "That's why you forgot."

"Don't talk like that, huh? What's wrong with you?" Nuno closed the door to the tiny bathroom. He couldn't piss, but he ran the water, washed his hands, splashed his face.

Outside, he climbed into the passenger side of his son's truck, but Paulo paused as he opened his door, looking across the yard. Catarina was outside her front door, crouching to examine the lantern that she kept there. Paulo muttered something to Nuno and then jogged across the yards suddenly, whistling and slapping his thighs.

Catarina stepped forward cautiously and shook Paulo's hand. Nuno's ears burned as he heard her laugh, and just like that something opened up inside of him and his heart pounded in his chest. Should he get out and walk over? Maybe one of them would turn around and wave him over. Nuno waited, but neither of them did. So he reached over and beeped the horn to get their attention, enjoying the way they both flinched.

Paulo started the engine, flicked the lights on, and slapped Nuno on the shoulder.

"How about going to Angelo's for Italian?"

"How is she?" Nuno couldn't help himself.

His son shook his head and grinned as they pulled out. "I tell you, Dad, if I wasn't married . . ." his voice trailed off. "You might have to teach me some Portuguese," he said, and smiled a strange half-smile. "I don't remember much."

Nuno felt himself trembling. They used to speak the language together, when Paulo was younger. Now it was only a few words here and there. "Never wanted to learn before."

"Never had a reason to," said Paulo.

Nuno held up his hand to signal to his son that the conversation was over.

Paulo started coming over more often. He never brought Claire; she had broken her ankle playing racquetball and her leg was in a cast. Nuno made up excuses sometimes so he could be alone, but Paulo still showed up. Sometimes his shiny silver GMC Jimmy would be there when Nuno got home, and he would find his son across the yard attempting to talk with Catarina, gesturing with his hands.

A few weeks later, Paulo sat across from him at the table, examining his fingernails, an empty High Life can open in front of him. He told Nuno that he and Claire weren't doing so well. "Look, Pop, we haven't been for a while," he said softly, "but, you know, then there's Scott to think about."

"You were happy once, no?" asked Nuno, "You'll be happy again." He cleared his throat. He wanted to tell Paulo that Catarina had been put here for *him*. Paulo had a wife, and even if she was quiet and frail, she was pretty, with blonde hair and pale skin. He didn't need Catarina. Nuno did. "Work it out," he said, tapping his hand on the table to accent each word. "Just work it out."

Paulo just stared at his father. He looked older to Nuno recently; his face seemed harder. "I'm trying," he said. "I'm trying."

But Nuno knew he brought Catarina things. There was a vase with flowers in one of the windows now, blocking his view. When they began to wilt, fresh ones appeared. He found some cellophane gift wrap in the trash in the kitchen once.

"Dad, how do I say let's go out to dinner in Portuguese?" Paulo asked one evening, tapping his father's shoulder as they stood admiring the garden. Nuno turned and walked back toward the house.

"I'm taking a nap," he said. "Go home, see Claire." He tried to keep his voice even. But he knew Paulo would wait for her. He watched through the window as his son helped bring in her groceries, his thick arms carrying four bags at once, and when Paulo went inside her house and closed the door behind them, Nuno lay down on his bed in the dark, his hands shaking ever so slightly. But he couldn't fall asleep.

—

On the first Wednesday in December, Sporting was to play AS Monaco, a French team. If they won, they would advance to the next round of the Champions League, something they hadn't done in seventeen years. There was a new poster of the team up at the club, and Luis had even typed out the standings neatly and pinned them next to it. Inside the club, as was tradition for a big game, there was more cold Sagres than wine. For some reason beer had always gotten to Nuno quicker than anything else. Sporting won easily, they would advance, and Luis poured shots of *aguardente* for all the men as they huddled around the bar and toasted. Nuno felt warm and hopeful, and he let himself get drunker than usual. He would go home and Catarina would be there.

Suddenly it came to him, and his heart quickened as he raised his glass and smiled to himself. Today he would not just watch her but go over and see her. He would speak Portuguese with her, maybe sit and eat some of the *bacalau* or *arroz de peixe* that she cooked, and they would speak of Lagos and Sintra.

On the way home, Nuno tasted the sweetness of the *aguardente* on his lips and felt it sizzle in his stomach. The dusk smelled different. December was coming, bringing earlier evenings and bitter cold air. Clouds drifted to hide the setting sun. And she was waiting for him. Not Helena standing sweaty and heaving at the stove, but Catarina, maybe walking lazily around the house, or lying upstairs in bed. He would go right in. Or would he knock? Weeks before, he had picked out a picture from years ago to show her; he was standing with two friends in front of the town square in Lagos, next to the sculpture of Dom Sebastião. He thought it would help with conversation. Doubt pinched his stomach for a second. Would she let him in? Just to sit with her, to talk to her, might be enough. Maybe she was lonely herself. Maybe he could help. He had never really even been able to picture making love to her, though he often tried. Once he thought about how it would be afterward, and how it used to be with Helena when they were young.

Something cold, Helena used to say when they were done, and he'd bring ice and put it on her stomach and they'd watch it slide down and melt, and then they'd do it again, wet and hot and cold.

Nuno parked his car in the driveway. Inside the house it still smelled of the rice he had burned the night before, the blackened pan waited for him on the counter. He moved quickly to the sink and the window above it. Parked crookedly in her small driveway, behind her pickup, was Paulo's truck.

This changed things. He felt the thin sliver of a headache already drumming in the back of his head. Rummaging through the cabinet, he found only an old bottle of port wine, which he sloppily uncorked and placed on the table. Then he changed his sweater and put on more deodorant—just in case—and found the glass he usually drank his orange juice out of in the morning.

Nuno sat at the table and drummed with his hands, the house feeling even more empty and quiet than usual. He drank a quick glass of the wine, which had a dusting of crumbled cork across the top. It was good though, and he wondered where it had come from. Why had they never opened it? Had Helena forgotten about it? Had she been she waiting for a special occasion? He poured more as the darkness crept across the yard. Now his wife was gone, and he was drinking the wine she had saved and dreaming about another woman. That familiar feeling of self-loathing pressed down on his shoulders, and he let it dig into him.

From time to time he peered over at Catarina's house through the window, but nothing had changed. He wasn't sure exactly when he realized that all the shades were pulled down.

The sound of Paulo's truck revving up woke him. Nuno's head had been resting on the table. His mouth tasted sour, his throat was dry. He thought he heard a jumble of voices and a door slamming, but it all echoed from somewhere far away. There was half a glass of wine poured before him, and he stared at it blankly.

Paulo's truck was gone. Nuno stood suddenly, blood rushing to his head, and then picked up his glass and finished it, his legs weak. How much time had passed? An hour? Two? He brushed his teeth and wet his hair, combing it into place, and patted the photograph in his pocket reassuringly. Then he took a deep breath and went out the screen door and across the shadows of the yard.

At the door Nuno paused, his heart hammering in his chest, trying to calm down. He held up his hand to knock, but then just stood there, his hair wet, his body tired. He could hear the hum of a television, and some high-pitched sounds he couldn't make out. The broad windows to his right were covered with blinds. On the steps next to him there was the old lantern made of glass that Catarina usually lit in the evenings. Sometimes he watched it flicker in the darkness and wished she was there next to him.

But he never saw her at night. It occurred to him that night was the only time that he never watched her. The only time she was free of him. Nuno felt ashamed suddenly. He slowly put his hands in his pockets and turned around. Maybe this wasn't right. He could feel his armpits growing damp, his fingers beginning to tremble in the cold. Small drops of rain had begun to spit down, grazing his skin. He could walk home, eat something, settle into his chair. Maybe tomorrow they would see each other outside. Maybe he would wave, or even say something. But not now. Not now.

But as he turned and began to shuffle down the stairs, he tripped. His arm shot out to catch himself but only bashed into the lantern, which toppled down the steps and shattered. For a second he lay there on his side, shocked in the silence, waiting. Then he heaved himself up, pain knifing his lower back, and forced himself to limp away, glass crunching beneath his feet.

Behind him, he heard the wooden door open and the screen door latch click. He stopped. The palm of his right hand throbbed where it had been cut. He squeezed it into a fist.

Catarina stood in the doorway. Her bathrobe was pulled tightly around her. She peered out, squinting her eyes, her mouth open. *"Alô?"* she said loudly. *"Alô?"*

The glass—she could cut her feet! "Stop there," Nuno heard himself saying hoarsely. *"Pare, pare,* stop!"

Nuno approached her cautiously. Even in the dimness, he could see that her face was red and pinched, that thin lines framed her eyes. Her damp hair curled around her shoulders, steaming slightly in the cold air.

"Nuno!" She stared at him searchingly, standing motionless. *"Cual é o problema?"*

Nuno stood before her, frozen. She remembered his name. Maybe she knew everything. *What if she'd seen him watching her?* Was he stupid to think that she hadn't? His hand was stinging, and he clenched his wet fist behind his back, gritting his teeth.

Catarina pointed at the glass that littered the steps. *"O que é isto?"* Her voice was sharp and accusatory. He noticed that her right eye was red and swollen.

Nuno swallowed, clutching the picture in his pocket with his good hand. His thoughts were coming too fast to catch them. It couldn't have been Paulo, could it, that did that to her? He tried to speak softly to her. *"Desculpe,"* he began. "It's okay. I'll help you. What happened?"

He started to climb the steps, his cut hand still tucked behind his back. They needed each other. Maybe it wasn't crazy. He could show her that he was a good man. Nuno smiled up at her and kept talking as she traced her fingers over her puffy eye, glaring down at him. "I'm sorry about—what happened. What happened? Paulo, he . . . it'll be all right."

At the mention of Paulo, Catarina stepped back into the house and out of the light rain, her arm braced against the door. "Paulo!" she snapped. *"Seu filho."* Her lip curled upward and her eyes gleamed. When the English words spilled out, they startled him. "Your son, this *asshole*? I don't want, I don't want anything from you—get out, Nuno, get out. Go! *Sai!*"

Nuno stopped, waiting for her to finish. But she never did. Instead, she kicked at some of the loose glass around her feet.

"I don't know what happened," Nuno said, his voice louder now as he labored over the words. "But you can tell me. Catarina, I'll do everything—anything for you. I've—I've always wanted to talk to you. You're so beautiful. I used to tell my wife. She loved you. And I have this picture to show you, and I can help you. I can. *Deixe-me ajudar.* Let me help."

He fumbled to pull the picture from his wallet, his hands still shaking, but nothing was coming out right. It was jumbled and wrong, not what he wanted to say at all. And Catarina was squinting accusingly at him, fiddling anxiously with the doorknob. She shook her head again and pointed back in the direction of his house. *"Desculpe,"* she said tiredly. "Please go."

She knew. Nuno took a shaky step backward, down the steps. He dropped the picture. It was suddenly clear to him. She knew about everything—the chairs, the blinds, everything. She knew.

He turned, his face burning, and began to walk gingerly away from her. Maybe she would call out for him to stop. Maybe she would reach down for the picture, before it was ruined by the rain. Maybe she would run after him.

But as he walked away, all he heard was the slam of the screen door and the click of the lock. The words were still forming in his mouth, the syllables still pouring out, but they felt strange somehow, foreign. Nuno kept whispering to himself as he walked across the wet grass, his feet aching in the cold, his ears ringing in the silence.

believe

Claire never thought that Paulo would actually hit her. And he hadn't *hit* her, she supposed. To be completely fair, he'd just *let her* fall down the stairs. He'd slapped his palms against her bare shoulders at the top of the stairs, and Claire pitched forward, missed the banister, and then rag-dolled down the steps. Her mouth popped open as she tumbled, but no sound came out. Her knee-jerk reaction to shock, to fear, had always been one of instantaneous silence, and this time was no different.

Then everything was still. Claire could feel the burn of the rug on her knees, the blood seeping slowly through skin. She gaped at its brightness. The tick of the wooden clock on the wall—a gift from Paulo's parents, years before—echoed loudly in the other room. Her hand was drawn to the back of her head like a magnet. There was a lump already.

Paulo said later that it looked as though she didn't even try to catch herself. That she'd just leaned forward and let herself go. Had she? He said that since Claire had never been able to ski or surf or rock climb or do anything where she would have learned *how* to fall, it made sense. So it wasn't all his fault, it definitely was not all his fault.

But Claire watched Paulo grow more and more animated, and motion with his hands, and she felt—how could she describe it?—very far away from him. She'd never *wanted* to do any of those things. She remembered watching him try to surf on their honeymoon in Hawaii. Fat white men with bulging stomachs and small Hawaiian children paddled and stood up effortlessly in the green waves, while Paulo wrestled against the big white board, the muscles in his shoulders flexing, his face red. Claire had silently cheered for him from the beach: *stand up, stand up*. But she wouldn't feel badly for him now if she saw him out there, the whitecaps crashing over his head so that he disappeared.

Move your foot, she told herself, lying there at the bottom of the stairs. *Move your leg, at least.* But her ankle was turned the wrong way, and it wouldn't listen to her. It didn't really hurt yet, just felt warm, inflated. It was only when Paulo reached down—his hands rough on her back, pulling her up—that everything began to ache.

The waiting room at Women's and Infant's Hospital smelled like urine and Lysol. Claire picked up *Vogue* but it was old and damp, with pages ripped out. Who would steal these pages, she wondered? She found the sex column and tried to read "The Best Places to Touch Your Man That You (and He) Never Knew About." It said that a man's thighs and the bottoms of his feet are erogenous zones that are often ignored. Claire wrinkled her nose at the thought of touching Paulo's cracked, sweaty feet. He'd look at her like she was nuts. Paulo never touched her feet; she didn't think he had ever considered her erogenous zones, or even knew what those were. Their routine was simple—he licked his finger and then stuck it into her for a few minutes to get her wet, then climbed on top of her and was done. Claire had given up on changing it. But lately he'd stopped doing even that, unless he was drunk. And lately, she'd found herself in the unfamiliar position of having to seduce *him*. She was a healthy, almost-middle-aged woman, after all—she had needs, too. And even though the sex wasn't the way it used to be, it was still . . . what was it? It was an escape, Claire decided. It was a few minutes where they could listen to their bodies and hopefully give each other what they wanted. I mean, she used to come *most* of the time with Paulo, which was pretty good, right?

Recently, though, he claimed he was tired or he wasn't feeling well. When they did do it, he closed his eyes more than he used to. Claire wondered if he was picturing someone else. She wondered, for a split second, if he could be having an affair. But who would want to sleep with him? I mean, she knew he was still handsome, but there was something different in his face now, in the lines in his forehead, that didn't used to be there. Or, maybe it didn't used to be as severe. If Claire met him now, not back when she was in her twenties, but now, she honestly wasn't sure that she'd go anywhere with him, even just out to dinner.

She kept skipping words and reading the same sentence over and over. The small black letters trembled on the page. She tried to block out the itching beneath the cast, but found herself wondering whether, if she got a hanger and bent it straight, she could shove it down there and scratch. Who cared if she broke the skin, even. Claire glanced around the room. Was there a closet or something? Was that a ridiculous question? Anything would be better than this sticky heat that felt as though mosquitoes were trapped inside the layers of the cast, buzzing and stinging.

When were they going to call her? The secretary had one hand in her mouth, playing with her gum. That was definitely not sanitary. She might as well stick it on the wall. Beads of sweat tickled Claire's forehead. There was absolutely no need for the heat to be blasting. Next to her, a woman with acne scars on her face slouched in her chair, coughing without covering her mouth. What did she have? Would they take this cast off today? Just *considering* that idea was half ecstasy, half torture. She put the magazine down and checked her phone, because lately on Fridays Paulo had been going out for a drink after work.

It was 5:35. Claire's appointment had been set for 5:15. She began to stare at the girl in the booth, who just snapped her gum and twirled her hair. Claire found herself wishing that that some of the gum would stick to her finger, then tangle in her hair. The woman next to her mumbled something under her breath and coughed again. What if she was contagious?

It was the way that Paulo looked at her lately, as if he was sizing her up, or maybe comparing her to someone else. Claire didn't think he was cheating, not yet at least. She'd be able to tell, she was pretty sure. But he was acting differently, that was for sure. If it was an affair, she'd have caught him. He was a terrible liar. But wasn't that what all wives probably thought—that they'd know? That for some reason, it'd be different if it was *their* husband?

Claire flipped absently through another magazine. Paulo was definitely drinking more, and that wasn't a good thing. They used to keep a few bottles of liquor in the cupboard, and they'd sit there for months, gathering dust. Lately, new bottles had been appearing. Claire didn't think that Paulo knew that she was aware of it, and she hadn't brought it up. She didn't even know when he drank, really. Before bed? When she was at the gym and he was watching a game or something? She couldn't even go to the gym with her ankle like this—maybe that was why her mind was so all over the place? It had kept her centered, the running and sweating, the music pumping into her ears as she pedaled. She loved the feeling that filled her in the car on the way home from a workout—that the rest of the day was full of possibility. If she was going to spend it by herself, then all the better.

And she probably would be. Paulo spent more time at that club now, that bar that his dad went to all the time. Sometimes when he came back, there was this nauseatingly sweet scent of liquor on his breath when he climbed into bed. He would never force her to do anything, but if she pulled away, and he was in the mood, his entire body stiffened up. Sometimes he punched the mattress or kicked the bed as she lay there, trying to drift away. He was just too tense these days, but Claire knew he'd always been tightly wound, always had a temper. Her older sister, who lived in San Diego, used to say that all Portuguese men had tempers, that it ran in their blood. Claire wasn't sure if her sister had really liked Paulo when they met, but they'd never really talked about it. It was awkward, really, an awkward thing to talk about.

Maybe part of what was going on lately had to do with his mother. Helena was getting close to the end, and Claire knew that everyone sensed it. She hadn't been over there in a while, but after his last visit, Paulo had come back pretty upset. He said that his mom would seem fine one minute, but then she'd just collapse into a chair, unable to catch her breath. She was overweight, she had smoked all her life, and she was getting old. But Nuno wouldn't put her in a nursing home. And the really sad thing was the way that Nuno looked at his wife. It was as if he'd already considered what his life would be like without her, and he wasn't willing to give her away yet. With every move she made, with her every deep, wheezing sigh, his eyes clung to her, as if holding her together.

Claire used to think that one day, Paulo would look at her like that. Now she wasn't so sure.

It was hard for her to watch Nuno and Helena, so she knew it was difficult for Paulo too. She tried to be understanding, though she'd never felt that Paulo's parents had really taken to her. Paulo used to get mad when she brought it up, but Claire was fine with it now. Neither of his parents had ever really treated her like one of the family. She never laughed at the right times, never felt comfortable when they would speak Portuguese and she couldn't understand. Sometimes, in the beginning, she'd wondered if they were talking about her. Paulo had always said that they loved her, that she was imagining things. "Claire, you're acting *crazy,*" he would say. But Claire knew that she wasn't. Over the last few months, she had been making up excuses and going over there less and less.

Claire leaned back and raised her ankle, trying to reposition it. It felt bloated. She wondered what it looked like under there. This was the first bone that she'd broken, and honestly, she hadn't thought the cast would be so heavy. Last night, she jerked awake out of a sound sleep, her foot white-hot with pins and needles, but Paulo was asleep and she didn't want to wake him. So she just lay there, one hand clutching her forehead, trying to stay calm as he snored. Trying to think of something, anything else. She didn't want to, but she kept thinking of how he pushed her, how he snapped his hands against her shoulders. That frightening feeling of losing control and pitching forward, not knowing how she would land. What would it feel like, she wondered, to just slap him across the face?

Claire never could. Last night, though, as she watched him sleep, she almost wanted to. Almost.

She wished she could stand up to him. She wished she could've pushed him back, or at least screamed until her throat was hoarse. To be honest, she didn't know why she couldn't. She liked to think that the ankle had changed things, had pushed her closer to saying something. She liked to think that it had changed Paulo, too. Claire hoped that she'd never need to push back, to shout, to raise her fists. That this was a one-time thing. That if he ever tried to hurt her again, if he ever laid his hands on her again, she'd pack her stuff and get out. She could call her sister in California. Or better yet, she could kick Paulo out. Call the police, throw the phone at him so it cracked him in the forehead and shook him out of it. She wouldn't do that. But she'd do *something*.

Something. Instead of just crying as she lay at the bottom of the stairs and he held her ankle in his hands, whispering for her to calm down. He had looked stunned for a moment. "You're fine," he'd said, "right? It's fine."

Of course he felt bad. But he looked more frightened than anything. "I *am* sorry, hon," he kept saying in the days that followed, "I really am."

Claire admittedly blamed some of it on herself. Maybe she should've seen it coming. When they'd first started dating, Paulo was a big drinker, and he'd get into these possessive, angry moods when he was drunk, ready to fight the first guy that laid eyes on her at the bar. She'd get mad at him of course, but sometimes, if she was drunk, too—and it only took a few glasses of wine—she'd shamelessly flirt with someone, anyone, just to set him off. She was young then, and she had to admit that it kind of excited her, to see him like that. And when they got home, he'd say the sweetest things, like telling her how all he wanted was to have a family of his own. As corny and stupid as it sounds, it felt like he was opening up his soul. It felt as though they needed each other. For a while, she thought they did.

And in the beginning, the sex *was* good. Granted, Claire hadn't experienced much. She'd been cautious, drawn to shy, gentle men who were scared to take control. But Paulo was different, and she never told him, but there was a small part of her that loved knowing that he had the will to actually fight for her. She could see it in the bright glare of his eyes when he was on top of her, his hands gripping the headboard.

But that glare dimmed when they had Scott. Claire knew Paulo wanted a son, but as Scott had grown older, it was almost as if he sucked some of the life out of Paulo. She felt strange to be thinking it, but with every year that passed, Scott looked more like Paulo—except for the blond hair he inherited from her—and Paulo seemed to almost *resent* him for it. Based on what Paulo had told her about himself in high school, Scott had become the person that Paulo always *wanted* to be, the most popular, a star soccer player even—so maybe Paulo felt as though he missed out. Or he was just jealous. He used to tell her that he never felt as though his father was proud of him, that he never lived up to being the son Nuno wanted. And she knew he didn't want to act that way with Scott. But maybe he couldn't help himself. Claire watched Scott roll his eyes when Paulo grilled him about soccer over the dinner table, about school, even about Hailey, Scott's girlfriend. But it was almost as though Paulo tried too hard now, with Scott, with her, with everything. And Claire had caught him staring at Hailey—I mean, she's beautiful, with strawberry-blonde hair and a body that's almost too mature for her, and she and Scott look great together—but Claire had also seen Paulo's eyes stay glued to those long legs for far too long.

Claire glanced back at the magazine on the table. "Secret Sex Tips!" read another headline on the cover. Maybe she needed to make more of an effort? Try harder to interest him, dress up for him, talk dirty? She imagined herself strutting through the bedroom in her cast and almost let out a wry laugh. She couldn't do any of that without a drink herself. However, that actually might be a welcome thing these days. Might help with the itching, too.

Claire also wondered if Paulo missed traveling. Before they started dating, he backpacked all over Europe and Brazil, some other places too. But it was weird how he never put up any of the pictures he had taken, even though she suggested that he frame them, or at least put them into albums. He'd rarely, if ever, talked about the time that he spent out of the country. Years before, when he had shown her the pictures that he kept in boxes under the bed, he went through them quickly and his eyes kind of glossed over.

Claire crossed and uncrossed her legs, exhaling slowly. She knew that Paulo was a good man. She wouldn't have married him if he wasn't. She'd always been aware that he was intense and passionate and temperamental, but it gave him an edge she liked. It was strange, she used to picture them living out their lives together—when Scott was older and had a family of his own—the way that Paulo's parents had. But now when she thought of the future, she saw blurry images that folded up and slipped away from her, like old Polaroids that you flip through but can't quite place. Sometimes she saw her sister, sitting out on her lawn in the sun, palm trees waving in the background, beckoning.

Claire pressed a hand to her forehead, then the back of her neck. Did she feel warmer than usual? She couldn't pretend to read the magazine anymore. From the cover some actress whose name she couldn't place grinned confidently at her. Why the hell couldn't she be in this cast instead of her? The room was empty now, silent except for the buzz of the fluorescent lights. The coughing woman was gone—Claire hadn't even noticed that she'd left.

She tried to move her ankle, squirming and flexing the muscles, but the itch grew so strong that she had to ball her hands into fists to keep from crying out. She dug her fingernails into her palms. She needed to tell the doctor about the itching. This couldn't be normal. Her stomach heaved, and she imagined, against her will, the inescapable horror and embarrassment of throwing up in this room, the splashing and heaving and cries of outrage from the bitchy woman in the booth.

Claire wished she were more religious, because she'd pray for the future of their marriage. But she'd never been, and Paulo wasn't anymore, either. She knew his parents were; there was a picture of Jesus, or a tiny statue, in every room of their house. She wondered what Jesus would do if he had this goddamn cast on his leg, itching like crazy. Would *he* be able to turn the other cheek?

God, was she losing her mind?

Claire wanted to believe Paulo yesterday when he'd tapped the cast with his empty beer glass and said that he wished every day it was on his foot, that he never thought she'd actually fall down. That he only meant to grab her and shake her and *hold onto her*, but she moved too quickly, too soon. She didn't think he was lying. She knew he was sorry.

"I wish I could get in there and scratch it for you," he'd said, shrugging. "I wish I could, hon."

Then he'd refilled his glass, smacked his lips, and taken a long sip. Claire had opened her mouth to speak, to say, You know what, Paulo? That wasn't what you were trying to do, not at all. You weren't trying to hold onto me. You're *not* trying to hold onto me. And if you are trying, you better try harder.

But she didn't say that. She didn't say anything.

almost gone

Tonight, for some strange reason, Claire had come out of their bedroom and just stood there behind the couch. Lying there, a blanket covering his bare feet, his right hand on his crotch, Paulo knew before he turned around that she was biting her lip with her crooked front teeth, and that her right hand was on her hip, playing with the thinning cotton of her old nightgown.

"Coming to bed?" she'd said meekly. The light from the TV flickered on her freckles.

But he couldn't. Not the way it was lately, with Claire nudging him with her long slender legs, rubbing against him as he tried to imagine that she was someone else.

He shook his head and glanced back to the screen. "I'm not tired yet."

But he knew that he'd spend the night on the couch, drinking tall cans of Pabst Blue Ribbon and watching reruns of *SportsCenter* until he was sure that the play would be made, until he'd memorized all the clever quips.

It wasn't Claire's fault. She had a delicate, pointed nose, thin blonde hair, and cream-colored skin that burned in the summertime. She was in great shape from toiling at the gym, but she was attractive in a way that just didn't appeal to him anymore. Even back when they used to make love regularly, Paulo covering her mouth with his hand so she wouldn't wake Scott, both of them laughing, he'd always pictured other girls. Even now, Paulo still found himself fantasizing about Isabella, his high school girlfriend, and that went back over twenty years.

He'd never had this much trouble sleeping, though. It could be the fact that he was drinking more, he supposed, but he knew deep down that it was Catarina.

The first time that Paulo saw her had been exactly one week earlier. She was walking around the old house behind his father's, bending down to look at the wildflowers that were dying in the cold of autumn. He'd known that someone was supposed to move into the house in September, and he'd seen a truck parked in the driveway a few times, but his father had never mentioned a woman. She didn't fit in back there amidst the dry brown grass and his father's small vegetable garden, in the backyard where Paulo had spent much of his childhood.

"Dad, who's your new neighbor?" Paulo asked, the door slamming behind him.

His father stood up to hug him, wincing at the noise. "From Portugal," he said flatly, dropping into his sagging brown armchair, squinting at the screen.

"Jesus, I know that. Have you met her? Have you talked to her?"

Nuno seemed surprised by the question. "No. Why would I?"

"Well, what's her name?"

Nuno sat up, rubbing his knees as if he was cold.

"Dad?"

"Catarina," said Nuno, standing, "her name's Catarina. Let's go eat, huh?"

"Catarina," Paulo repeated softly as he followed his father out the front door.

By the time he'd seen her twice, Paulo had become fascinated. He wondered what her house looked like. What her voice sounded like. What color her skin was under her sundress. He envisioned her as a passionate, strong-willed woman, and it excited him.

There had been plenty of women when Paulo was younger, starting in high school, and then afterward as he traveled. His parents had come from Portugal, but he'd been born in the States, and grown up here. After high school he'd begun working right away—landscaping in the summer, factory work in the winter—helping his parents but also saving money so he could go backpacking. Brazil had been his favorite; he'd found it easy to get around, meet interesting people, sleep with women. He'd never made it to Portugal, though he'd wanted to go, and he got the sense that his father had wished he had.

Paulo was twenty-four and living alone in Rhode Island when he met Claire. They married after six months of dating and quickly had Scott, in part because Claire was a few years older than he was and worried about getting pregnant too late. Paulo felt ready to be done traveling, he was thrilled to have a son, and his parents were finally happy. Everything felt right, at first. He loved Scott fiercely, and he loved Claire, too. But looking back, he wasn't sure he'd *ever* felt the way he had after just *seeing* Catarina that first time—the reaction was so immediate, so sharp, it was as if she'd cut him and the wound wouldn't heal.

Tonight, thinking about Catarina made him feel slightly guilty, so Paulo went to join Claire in bed. He listened to the pages of her book turn, finding it difficult not to despise the habit she had of touching her finger to her mouth before turning each one. He waited for her to sigh the way she did every night, the small contented breath that he found so irritating lately. Finally, she closed the book, clicked the tiny reading light off and tucked herself next to him so that their legs were lightly touching. Under the blanket her cast made a swollen lump.

Claire whispered something he couldn't make out just as he was drifting off. He slowly pulled his leg away from hers. She shifted and her hand settled lightly on his chest. He turned away slowly, thinking that she could be asleep, or close to it. She wasn't like him; she could drift off in an instant, anywhere, at any time.

But her hand moved. Now it was on his stomach. He was aware of the warmth of her breath on his bare skin. Now her hands traced down lightly, reaching.

Paulo slowed his breathing and stayed perfectly still, waiting for her to stop. Pretending, as he did when he was a teenager. He pictured the ocean brushing against the shore, and on the beach next to him lay Catarina, her dark skin glistening with saltwater.

In the morning Claire pretended nothing had happened. They sat across from each other at the small, cracked wooden table and passed the *Providence Journal* back and forth.

"We're out of sugar," Paulo said, putting the cover back on the empty silver bowl.

"I'm going shopping tomorrow," Claire said. "When will you be home tonight?"

Paulo paused and sipped his coffee. "I'm so tired lately. I wonder if I'm getting sick."

"What time?"

"What? Oh, I don't know. I have lots to do at work, then I told my dad I'd visit him. Maybe stay for dinner."

Claire put down the lifestyles section and looked at him. Always the lifestyles section she reached for first, or the arts, as if there was nothing going on in the world. Paulo went for the sports first only if he thought there might be something about Scott—a goal, an assist, a feature article like last week. Any other time it was the front page. Because there were bad things happening every day, worse than he could imagine, and sometimes reading about them made him feel better about his own life.

"Is Scott up yet?" he asked.

Claire nodded and stared at him as she reached down and scratched at her cast. "Really itchy today," she said under her breath.

What the fuck. How many times did he have to apologize? It wasn't on purpose. He'd rushed her to the hospital right after it happened, as the ice he'd wrapped around her foot dripped all over the floor of the car. He hadn't known she would trip and go all the way down the steps, had he?

"Thank God Scott is away," was the only thing that she had said to him that entire night. Scott had been visiting a friend in New York for the weekend, and by the time he'd returned, they had their story straight. Claire even admitted she understood, and that was what disgusted Paulo the most.

"You can get mad at me," he told her. "It's normal. It's all right."

But she hadn't. And looking at her now as she smiled wanly at something that she saw in the comics, he didn't think she ever would.

"I have to get ready for school," she said. In the sunlight, her blonde hair shone as if it was translucent, and there were faint dark circles under her eyes. She put her head down on the table for a moment.

"I don't feel like going today," Claire said softly. "Why do I have to go?" Paulo had gone into her classroom a few times when they were first dating, and he'd been amazed by how strong her voice sounded, the way the children clung to her legs as she walked.

"What if we visit your father on Sunday, and tonight you come home?" she whispered.

He stared down at his coffee. There was a spiral of thin, faint white ripples as he stirred. The milk could be spoiled.

"Please?" she said, and that did it.

"No," he said and stood up and reached for his coffee cup. "No can do, Claire."

—

Paulo drove a delivery truck for a liquor distributor. He was always running late, stuck behind too many red lights, his heart pounding from drinking too much Dunkin' Donuts coffee. His clients affectionately called him LP, Late Paulo, and while he laughed when they said this, inside he seethed, resolving never to be on time again.

Friday afternoon he spent the last two hours of his day unloading box after box of beer and liquor outside Mcgrath's Package Store. An hour later he drove to Scott's school, South Kingston High, and walked toward the soccer fields with his hands in his pockets.

Standing there alone, watching the sun hang lower and lower in the fading November sky, Paulo blew on his hands and felt his mind settle down. He concentrated on the movement of the ball and the shadows stretching across the field until finally there was a break and Scott ran over to him.

"Dad?"

"Hey, you guys are looking good," Paulo said, raising his hand for a high-five.

Scott looked back at the group of boys greedily drinking water and lounging in the grass and then tapped his father's hand reluctantly. "It's just practice," he said. "Why are you here, anyway?"

"I'm headed over to Grandpa's in a few. You want to come?"

Scott appeared not to have heard. He watched the team jog back onto the field. "Dad, I gotta go. Where's Mom?" He reached down and yanked at his shin guards.

"She's at home," Paulo said. "So I'll wait for you and we'll go eat with Grandpa?"

Scott shook his head and started to back away. Paulo heard someone call out Scott's name. "I'm going out with Hailey," he called out. "I'll see you tomorrow."

Paulo nodded and watched Scott join the game. He immediately received the ball and ran with it, gracefully slaloming through two defenders and then passing. Scott was naturally talented, none of it from him. Paulo felt the same pang he felt whenever he watched Scott play. He'd never been this good, not even close.

Scott was laughing now at something the coach was saying, running to the other side across the crackling brightly covered leaves. Paulo knew tonight his son would bring Hailey home to his room, quietly walk up the stairs, muffling giggles and wet kisses, and have sex with her in their house. He knew this because last Friday he couldn't sleep and he heard everything—zippers coming down, heavy breathing, Hailey's belt hitting the floor—the one she wore constantly, with the thick silver buckle—as Claire snored next to him. Hailey had reddish-blonde hair and dimples, and Paulo didn't want to listen, but there was nothing else he could do.

"Like that," Hailey had said, her voice not halted or whispered but matter-of-fact, "slower. No, slow. Like that."

⟶

On the way to his father's house Paulo stopped at the Ocean Mist for a drink. It was Friday, after all. He loved going to the Lusitania Club during the week, and sometimes on the weekends, to watch games and bullshit with Luis, the old bartender who'd been there forever, but he also liked going to the Mist lately, alone.

The place smelled of stale beer, and the rotting wood floor that creaked in spots. The bartender—Paulo thought his name was Andy—nodded to him and pulled a beer. "Lots of deliveries this week?" he asked.

Paulo took a large sip, then another. "'Course."

"You gonna be on time, LP?" Andy chuckled, but when Paulo didn't say anything, he stopped and leaned back against the bar, crossing his arms and looking away.

Paulo walked toward the small tables near the window that overlooked the Atlantic. "You know it," he finally called out, shaking his head. He watched Andy disappear into the kitchen, smirking. How the hell did he know about that? He drank rapidly. He'd need another soon. Outside, the swells were climbing higher and higher, washing over the rocks. Out past the breakwater, surfers in black wetsuits ducked under the crashing white foam.

"Kids are crazy, huh?" Andy said, wiping down a table behind him. "It's almost dark."

Paulo nodded. "Crazy," he said, peering through the glass, watching a skinny boy drop down the face of a wave and be blown sideways, disappearing as his surfboard spiraled in the air.

But it didn't seem crazy. Paulo signaled for another beer. He should be out there. He'd even tried surfing before, when he and Claire honeymooned in Waikiki. He doubted Claire even remembered. He'd been pissed because she'd missed the one good ride he'd gotten. It had definitely been harder than he'd thought, and the waves had been pretty big out there. When he'd come back to the beach, Claire had her eyes closed. She wasn't even watching him.

Sitting there, Paulo pictured himself out there in the swells, paddling to outrace walls of whitewater, the tops of the waves beginning to tear apart like huge sheets of paper ripping in the wind.

⁓

Paulo walked up the short flight of stairs and let himself in. There were a few dishes in the sink, a rumpled newspaper carefully refolded on the table. He could hear the familiar rise and fall of frenzied Portuguese from the television in the living room, the repetition of names as the ball was passed. Since his mother's death it always smelled musty in his father's house, and he cracked the window over the sink, suddenly picturing his mom standing at the stove, her wiry hair sticking up haphazardly, stirring a giant pot of rice. He hadn't spent enough time with her as she grew older, and with that thought he opened the fridge and searched for a beer.

"Dad," he called out. "Dad?"

With his father there was always something to talk about, even if it was only soccer, but before she died, his mother and Paulo had often sat in silence while he ate what she'd cooked. It was as if they'd run out of things to say to each other, and half the time Paulo didn't think she'd understand what he wanted to tell her anyway. It was strange, the way things had changed. When Paulo was younger, he had preferred his mother and shied away from Nuno, who he was a little bit scared of.

It was growing dark, and through the window Paulo could barely see Catarina's clothesline flapping in the wind. He squinted to see if he could make out what was hanging there. Dresses, shirts, jeans. Nothing too exciting.

"Dad?" he called out again from the foot of the stairs. "You hungry?"

Paulo went upstairs, passing dusty, framed pictures of himself. On one small table, the pictures were all face down, and he stopped to right them. Helena, Nuno, and a great-aunt who he didn't remember all stared back at him.

The door to his father's room was slightly ajar, and he knocked as he pushed it open. Near the window, Nuno was slouched awkwardly on the bed, and he whipped his head around toward Paolo. His face was red.

"What are you doing, taking a nap?" said Paulo.

"I was—"

"I thought we were going for dinner? You okay?"

"I'm fine. I guess I forgot. Didn't hear you come in." Nuno avoided Paulo's eyes and eased himself into the hallway.

Paulo pushed aside an empty chair and raised the blinds, which were halfway down. "Jesus, it's so fucking dark in here. That's why you forgot."

"Don't talk like that, huh? What's wrong with you?" Nuno muttered, closing the door to the bathroom, but Paulo ignored him. The view of Catarina's house from up here was much better, pretty much flawless, and the lights in her house illuminated each room clearly. Paulo watched, transfixed, as Catarina slipped out of her front door and walked out to her car.

"Let's go for dinner," Nuno called as he headed downstairs, the toilet flushing.

Outside, Paulo saw Catarina standing on the front steps of her house, facing the door. "Dad, hold on one second," Paulo said, and was surprised by the sudden flash of annoyance on his father's face.

He trotted toward the tiny house, his keys jingling in his hand, and as he got closer, he called out to her. "Hello," he said, "hello?"

Catarina turned toward him, her hand still on the key inserted into the lock. Her hair was in a long ponytail, and she wore a loose wool sweater. Paulo judged her to be in her early thirties, the slight lines in her forehead offsetting the swell of her breasts. She waved cautiously and stepped back against the door, running a hand through her bangs.

"Boa noite," she said, greeting him in Portuguese.

The familiar words chimed in his ears. He pointed to his chest and then jerked his hand at his father's house. "I'm Paulo," he said nervously. "That's my father's house back there."

She nodded as if she understood, but he wasn't sure. Then she turned her attention back to the key, jiggling it as if trying to free it.

"May I?" He reached out and she shrugged, then took her hand off the key. "Locked out?" he asked, grinning.

"It's . . . too tight," she said, and shook her head in frustration.

Suddenly there was a blast of the horn behind them, and they both jumped. Paulo glared across the dark yard at his car. "Sorry," he said, wiggling the key violently now, back and forth, "we're going to dinner, see." They both heard it click, and he turned it easily.

"There we go," he said.

"Obrigada," she said, pushing the door open.

"Nice to meet you," he said and stuck out his hand. Did she know any English at all?

She stared at it, and then took it in hers, not shaking it, just grabbing onto it for a second. Her skin was dry and rough.

"Maybe I'll see you soon," Paulo blurted out, and she cocked her head sideways, raising one eyebrow. He wracked his brain, but the only phrases that popped into his head were soccer-related. How could he not remember anything? "Um, I like you," he said finally in Portuguese. It was the only thing that he could think of. She stepped past him into the house, one hand covering her mouth, and Paulo thought for a second she might be laughing at him.

"Obrigada," she said as she closed the door. "Thank you."

At the restaurant the waitress smiled hopefully and smoothed the red and white checkered tablecloth. "Father and son, right?" she said to Paulo right away. "How cute you both are!"

Paulo looked at his dad and laughed, but Nuno barely smiled, just nodded. He was wearing an old blazer that Paulo had not seen on him in years. Over the last few weeks, Paulo had noticed that Nuno had begun combing his hair neatly and dressing better. He'd also noticed that his accent had gotten stronger. Maybe it was all the time he spent at the club now. The old-timers rarely spoke English down there.

"I think this is really going to be Scott's year," said Paulo, shoving a piece of bread into his mouth and refilling his glass of wine. "Junior year is an important one, you know? And he's playing better than ever. Did you read the article I told you about in the paper? I have it at home if you want."

Nuno nodded and his eyes lit up. Lately, the only time that Nuno perked up and talked as much as he used to was at Scott's soccer games. "Every game I come to, you score," he'd said proudly to Scott after the game last Friday.

But Paulo grew uncomfortable with the clouds of silence that gathered between his father and himself lately. He couldn't decide what Nuno was thinking about when he touched the tiny scar on his bottom lip—the one he'd gotten playing soccer when he was young—or when he stared blankly out the car window. Maybe he was thinking of Helena. They would have never gone out to eat before she died—it was a waste of money, and Helena's food was much better, anyway. The day after she passed, Paulo remembered scrubbing the burnt rice that Nuno had attempted to cook out of a pot, as people moved in and out of the house as quiet and faceless as shadows.

When Paulo dropped his father off, Nuno lifted himself slowly from the car, groaning softly. "Ate too much," he said. *"Boa Noite."*

"I'll see you at the game. Remember, it's on Sunday, not tomorrow like usual, Dad," Paulo said, craning his neck to see Catarina's house, where a few lights were still on. He thought he could hear a radio playing faintly. When he left, he circled around the neighborhood so he could drive past her house one more time, checking himself as the car began to drift sideways. He wished he could knock on her door, bring her flowers, dinner, something. Instead he drove home.

Paulo poured Jack Daniels over ice, sat on the couch, and punched buttons on the remote aimlessly.

Upstairs, he could hear Scott asking Claire what to wear on his date with Hailey. Their laughter buzzed in his ears, annoying him. There was nothing on TV, so he paged through the newspaper, reading only the headlines.

"Paulo, honey, could you come up here for a second?"

He pretended not to hear, leaned back, and brought the paper up to cover his face. He considered sleeping on the couch tonight. Then he thought of Scott bringing Hailey home and sneaking past him. Your parents are weird, she might say.

"Paulo? We need you for a second up here!"

"Mom, forget it," he heard Scott protest. "Forget it."

Paulo closed his eyes and took a long sip of whiskey. Maybe he could change things. Maybe he could go up there right now, laugh with them, and when Scott left, sit next to Claire and watch a movie. Rub her feet like he used to when she came home from work, tell her he loved her. Tell her he waited all week for this. Later they could put all the couch cushions on the floor and make love like they used to in the dim light from the TV, their clothes in a heap next to them, the cushions sliding beneath them on the wooden floor.

⁓

There was something touching his face. He had been dreaming of something, but it disappeared. His mouth was chalky and his back ached.

" . . . and you just kept sleeping, and Scott left, and I sat next to you for a while. You were snoring and you wouldn't wake up, and I thought, well, I'll just let him sleep, so I had some wine . . ." Claire belched and then giggled. "A lot of wine actually, and then—"

"What time is it?" Paulo muttered, rubbing his eyes and sitting up. Claire grinned hopefully, her face flushed.

She awkwardly lifted the foot with the cast over his lap and straddled him. "We haven't done this in so long," she said, undoing his belt.

"Umm . . ." he mumbled, his hands on her legs, "Claire, stop a second, I don't—"

She shook her head and unzipped his fly. "It's okay," she whispered; "it's okay." He had never seen her like this. He tried to push back, but she nuzzled his neck and his chin. He didn't want to, at all. It didn't feel good. He closed his eyes and leaned back, trying to picture someone else, but everything was fuzzy and soft and blank. What was wrong with him?

"C'mon," she whispered, "please, honey."

"Stop," he said, feeling suffocated under her weight. "Get off!" Paulo tried to stand, but she threw her arms around his neck, pulling down, so that when he stood she dangled from his shoulders. "Stop!" he cried hoarsely, his neck bending painfully. He grabbed her arms and yanked them apart, and she fell onto the floor on her back, exhaling when she hit. Her face grew dark red and she rolled onto her stomach, wheezing, her nightgown bunched around her waist, her bare legs askew, the cast around her ankle yellow in the light. She wasn't wearing any underwear.

"Claire?" he said, standing over her. "Claire?"

She wouldn't look at him but instead turned back over, coughing quietly, lying on her stomach with her face in her hands. "I'm sorry," she said finally. "I've had too much to drink."

Paulo looked down at her and then walked to the door. He hesitated with his hand on the knob, closing his eyes, waiting.

"Please don't leave," she said, turning slowly onto her side. "Paulo?"

The door clicked shut behind him. It was quiet outside, and the grass was wet with dew. When he started the car, he inhaled deeply and opened all the windows to let the cold air in.

Paulo woke up Nuno to tell him that he needed to sleep on the couch because Claire and he were having a little fight. Nothing serious, he said, and his father nodded, his eyes puffy and half closed. Once Paulo heard the sound of his raspy snoring echoing through the house, he carefully let himself out into the yard.

Catarina's house was completely dark. He searched for the light of a candle or a television, but there was nothing. He looked at his watch. Five past one.

Paulo heard a plane pass overhead, watched the lights blink across the clear sky. He sat down on the front steps of his father's house and looked again at the dark house before him.

After a few minutes, he stood up and walked back across the yard toward Catarina's. Even if he wanted to, he didn't think he could stop himself. Without hesitating he turned the doorknob, waiting for the sudden resistance of the lock.

But the knob turned. Her house was open. His heart sped up, and he swallowed. He stood there for a minute, wondering what to do, if she was there, if she was alone. He remembered the way that she had touched his hand.

Catarina's house smelled of seafood and perfume. He touched the walls with his hands, concentrating on the movement of each small step. It was almost completely black, except for the small green numbers on the microwave. When he found the banister with his hand, he ascended the stairs lightly, and at the top he paused. His eyes had adjusted and he could make out shapes now. The door to her room was open. The muffled sounds of her breathing floated like wisps of smoke.

If she wakes up I'll run, he thought. If she sees me I'll never come here again, I'll avoid her. Every thought felt exaggerated, as if he was dreaming. Maybe he was.

Paulo stopped at the doorway. Catarina slept on her side, one bare arm hanging off the bed. The air was heavier in her room, as if made that way by her presence. Her breathing was even louder than he had thought, her nose making rippling noises, her chest rising and falling, covered loosely in a thin sheet. He inched forward. Next to her bed, on the night table, was a bottle of pills. What did she take? Sleeping pills?

Paulo tried to breathe with her, in the same slow rhythm. After a moment, he watched his arm slowly stretch toward her bare shoulder. It moved closer and closer, until he could feel the electricity running under her skin. Until he could touch her if he just moved a finger.

Then he stopped.

Paulo remembered a game that his mother and he had played when he was very young. He would lie very still, waiting for her to tuck him in. Pretending to be asleep. When she came in, he would hold out as long as he could as she sat on the edge of the bed, watching him pretend until he burst out laughing.

"You almost fooled me," she'd say, kissing him goodnight. It had taken years and years of listening to his parents yell at each other to recognize that her cheeks were always wet when she kissed him, that her hands were often shaking as she leaned down to tuck his sheets around him. As she pressed her head against his.

Paulo pictured Claire lying in bed alone, anxiously waiting for the sounds of his car in the driveway. He thought of Scott and Hailey, naked together, each move they made shocking in its newness. He wondered if, this time, Claire was listening.

Back outside, the door clicking shut behind him, Paulo walked toward his car in the fleeting darkness, his hands in his pockets. The neighborhood was silent. It was time to go home. He didn't need to sleep at his father's. His stomach growled. Maybe he could pick up breakfast on the way, bring something home for everyone as a surprise. He'd gone out for a drive, to think about things, and that was that. Now he was back. Claire would wake up in a fog, her head aching, and clamber into the bathroom to get ready for the day. Scott would sleep the morning away and then wander downstairs at noon, stretching, starving.

Maybe some things could be changed. Erased, or ignored. Paulo twisted the key and his truck turned over, and then roared to life. The edges of the sky were turning from black to blue, the stars were disappearing. As he pulled away in the early morning light, Paulo switched the headlights on, just to make sure that he wouldn't miss anything.

smile

HAILEY · 2010

To: Scott777@hotmail.com
From: Hai175@yahoo.com

Dear Scott,

It's hard to write this. I guess I'm just going to do the best I can. Maybe you'll let me know your address soon, and I can send something snailmail. For now, this will have to do.

There's a lot I've been thinking about, obviously. I know you probably don't want to hear about all of it, but Dr. Rich thinks this is a good idea. She's been awesome, Scott. Before you were gone, since you've been gone. Talking to her is so good for me. She's given me some stuff for my depression and my anxiety, too, so I'm doing better. Anyway, we both thought that with the New Year passing and all, this would be the right time for me to get in touch with you, and get some things off my chest.

I have some journal pages here on my lap—'member that journal you got me for Christmas two years ago, with the cool cover? I've been writing in it every night. Sorry if there are some mistakes, but you know I'm not a good speller! I hope this isn't too hard for you to read. I do miss you (I hope you know that!) and I wish you'd come home. But I have to get this out. So here goes.

They wouldn't even let me touch her when I finally saw Emily at the beach. I was out looking for both of you all night. I don't know if you know that—how I drove around all night with the cops? This was after the hospital called and the nurse kept asking where you were, if I knew. She started *yelling* at me. "Do you know what your husband did? Jesus, do you even know? What kind of people are you?" And my reaction was honestly like "Fuck you, lady! You have no right!"

When I called the police, I remember while I was on the phone I knocked my coffee mug off the counter and it was like it dropped in slow motion. Then it shattered. I got picked up in the cop car with the lights flashing and all the neighbors looking at me as if I'd done something wrong. Like it was *my* fault. I can't even describe what was going through my head at that point, Scott. It was like it just went blank.

Do you realize that I didn't even get to hug her one last time? When we found her lying there in the sand, I put my hand against her cheek and it was so cold and wet that I almost threw up.

And you just sat there. I spun around, asking everyone, "Why is she wet? Why is she wet?" And I felt you watching me, Scott, sitting next to the lifeguard chair, shivering and watching me. But I didn't want to comfort you or help you. And you didn't look like you wanted me to, that was the thing. You didn't even look like you knew I was there.

Dr. Rich says that people step outside of themselves in moments that are too difficult to take. But that's not what I did. I didn't go anywhere. I was *there*. I screamed at you to make sure you looked at her. To make you *see*.

I hate to say this, but I need to. It felt *good* when I scratched you. It was like I finally got through to you. Then I saw the blood on your cheek, and the cops grabbed me. That big guy put his arms around me and his breath smelled like coffee. "Easy," he said. "Easy does it, ma'am."

Sometimes I think that none of it matters anymore. I wish I knew what you thought of all this, but I can't talk to you. Which is insane, that I can't talk to my own husband. Emily's gone, and now you're gone too. Disappeared. That's what people say, you know. Everyone says that. That you've *vanished*. I'm sure you'd love to hear that. You were always proud about how smart you were—remember that party we had for you when you graduated? I felt really bad that day. But I tried not to show it. I just wish I'd never had to drop out. It doesn't matter now, but God, there are so many things like that I never told you! Do they even matter now? I don't know. I hope they do.

You made sure you were the last one to see Emily, though, and that wasn't fair. You got to hold her, to hug her before she was gone. I got to run through the sand to our spot, crying, *freaking* out, and then see her spread out on the ground, her skin blue.

Do you know how much I tried to help you, afterward? I guess I thought that if we still had each other, we could try to go on. It sounds overdramatic now, I guess. At first I was worried that you'd be in trouble, that you could go to jail. But the lawyer helped. Then I found Dr. Rich, and started spending afternoons with her. Remember you came to the first session and then just bolted?

It's gotten better since you left, though, the therapy. I'm glad I didn't listen to you. You're not right about everything. Now we talk about your disappearance a lot. Also, what Dr. Rich calls your "obsession with Emily." And my "unresolved feelings" for her. Whatever. I know it sounds weird, like something we would have made fun of before.

She asked me the other day if I was ever jealous of Emily. I wanted to smack her. But you know what? I've been thinking about it a lot. Maybe I was jealous. It's normal, she says, for a mother to feel like that when her husband acts the way you did. She says it's not my fault. She says that you were too attached, that you ignored me, and that was part of the problem. It goes back to your parents and your upbringing, she says. I'd explain it if you were here . . .

Hey, I hope you're still reading, though! This is good for both of us, OK?

Do you remember how happy we used to be? It sounds so stupid, but I loved watching you play soccer when we first started dating. Remember how after you scored you'd point at me and smile? You'd do anything for me back then. And when I got pregnant and dropped out of URI during junior year, I was still so proud. Remember you'd press on my stomach to feel the kicking? You'd roll a soccer ball around my belly and say that our baby was going to be the best player in the world.

But everything started to fall apart when Emily got sick. It's OK to say that, Scott. It wasn't my fault, and I'm not blaming her. But it was the way you were with her. If she coughed, you jumped out of your seat to rub her back. Or put your ear to her chest. You slept on the floor of her room at night, and in the morning, your back ached so much that you walked with a limp. You'd spend hours on the phone with the doctors, comparing opinions. You even started buying those medical journals and taking books out of the library. We stopped going out to dinner and to movies, and when I brought it up, you'd shake your head. "How could you ever you sit through a movie when our daughter is in the hospital?" I can still hear your voice.

Dr. Rich says that that was our biggest mistake. She says we "never came up for air." Especially you. You never did. And I know I started drinking more. (OK, I know it became a problem and I'm saying right now, I'M SORRY, But Dr. Rich says that it's a coping meckanism that a lot of people use. I don't drink like that anymore. I didn't even have a drink on New Year's Eve, if you can believe that.)

But remember we used to have a few beers and then watch stupid TV shows and maybe end up making out on the couch? Sometimes we'd just fall asleep together, my head on your stomach. But when Emily got sick, you wanted to stay sober, you said, in case she needed you. I could see you silently counting how many glasses of wine I had. But after she was gone, you did a complete 180. Remember after you left Dr. Rich's office I found you at home drinking Jack Daniels from the bottle? Mumbling to yourself?

The way you acted about Emily just made me feel worse. Almost like I didn't *care* as much as you. We'd fight and then make up, but instead of us making love like we used to, you'd kiss my forehead and I'd sleep alone.

I'd lie there and hear you reading to her when she couldn't sleep, or telling her the story about your grandfather that she loved. How he scored two goals with a broken ankle back in Portugal. You even bought her those pajamas with soccer balls on them that said "Kick in Your Sleep" in big pink letters. She never took them off, since she never left the bedroom, and they got all dirty and gross, remember?

She wanted to take them to the hospital that morning, remember? But I didn't want people to think I'd let her go out like that. "Hailey," you said, "just let her take them. Just let her." But I ran out and bought her two new pairs instead. She didn't like them. I could tell by the way she held them up to her, and then glanced at you, her eyebrows raised. You walked out of the room and I cried that day for an hour. I bet you didn't know that.

I went to the hospital too, remember? Emily got pale and skinny and sometimes it was hard to look at her, but watching you was even harder. You acted happy but you weren't. You told me you were doing it for her but I think we *both* saw right through it. You'd do card tricks for her that had taken hours to learn, you brought balloons, flowers, candy that she wasn't supposed to eat. I couldn't get your laughter out of my head, and I don't know how Emily didn't notice. It was like nails on a chalkboard.

But you know what, Scott? I found a receipt from the bookstore in Wakefield for a Lonely Planet travel book on Brazil. And I re-checked the purchases on all our cards and found the plane tickets. You weren't too careful. I wonder sometimes if you wanted me to follow you. But how am I supposed to know, Scott?

Sometimes when I can't sleep, I get out of bed in the middle of the night and decide to just go. I've looked at pictures of Rio online, even found some great deals on tickets. I bought a suitcase and packed it with bathing suits and tank-tops. I keep it next to my bed with my passport. I haven't told Dr. Rich about my plans, because who knows if I'll ever go? She'd say not to. But I might. I really might.

I've made it as far as the airport. I sat in a bar at TF Green and had a drink and smoked half a pack of Parliaments. Then I went home.

I don't know, maybe it's my fear of flying, or how far away Brazil is. How would I find you in a city that it says online has 6,211,000 people?

But OK, this is the last thing. It's the way that I saw you look at me that day. It's something I try not to think about. For just a second, there was something in your eyes. Something that I never thought I'd see. But when I get nervous or overwhelmed, my body—my face—just reacts. It's my way of dealing with things, my way of protecting myself. Dr. Rich says I shouldn't feel bad about it. But I do. I want you to know that. I do.

Scott, I'll never forget the way the EMT used his thumbs to slowly close Emily's eyes. But I'd already seen them. Her eyes were clear and blank, and you know what I couldn't stop thinking about, which was so weird? We used to have staring contests, before she got sick. We'd hold our faces really close to each other, trying not to laugh.

OK, I think that's enough for tonight. I miss you and still love you so much and I still have a lot of hope for us.

I hope you read this.

Please read it.

XOXO

Hailey

just one night

NUNO · 1975

Nuno squeezed the letter so tightly that his hand shook. A loose wave of dizziness hit him, and he leaned against the wall. All around him, Helena's old dresses hung silently, like old ghosts.

He'd been digging through cardboard boxes, looking for that picture, the drawing that Helena had done of him playing football long ago. Paulo was trying out for the team next week, and Nuno was going to tack it up in his room, surprise him with it.

But the letter had found him first, folded neatly and tucked inside of a small wooden jewelry box. That was the thing too; it wasn't crumpled up, but put away carefully. The letter was from Mateo. After all of these years, it was really written in the way that Nuno had imagined he would write it—like a damn woman. There were hearts drawn on the side of the page, and even the faded letters were curly.

Nuno closed his eyes and everything came back. The sight of Mateo's pale face on the bed, the sand all over the blankets. How Nuno had crept away alone, leaving Helena there. She hadn't seen him, he was sure of that. And he'd never told her that he was there that night. He'd tried, in the days that followed, but he hadn't been able to. And slowly, the days and months and years piled over it, bringing a home thousands of miles away, and children, and new worries and problems. But that awful guilt had followed him everywhere, hadn't it? There was no escaping it. Nuno tried to breathe deeply, tried to calm himself down, but it was no use. He slumped against the wall and waited for the nausea to pass. Thank God Helena wasn't home.

He knew he wasn't innocent. Sure, it scared him. But he'd lived a long life already. He'd done good things and bad. He still believed in God, but he wasn't really sure what happened when people died. What would happen to him. But what was done was done. There was no going back, that was for sure.

Finally, Nuno opened his eyes and pushed his feet forward. How long had he been standing in this goddamn closet? It was dumb, really, all of it. There was nothing he could do. The past was the past. Helena would be home from Mass soon. There was still half the lawn to mow, and he'd left a cold beer on the counter. He put everything back in the box the way it was, shoved it into the shadows, and closed the door.

But as he walked downstairs, everything felt sucked of color. The sunlight poured through the windows, but it was ugly, heavy, and hot. Nuno swigged his beer, but it was warm. He poured it down the sink, watching the foam disappear. For the first time in thirty-four years, he felt different. About everything. He wasn't what had changed. But something was off.

When Helena pulled into the driveway, Nuno was sitting at the kitchen table, his usual spot. The door slammed, and he heard her talking to herself. He worried more about her driving alone lately. Her knees and ankles were tight with arthritis, and she didn't pay enough attention to the road. She was stubborn, though. She still insisted on driving to the few places that she went to frequently—church, the doctor's office, the supermarket, Paulo's school—and she wouldn't take no for an answer. Sometimes Nuno wondered if the medication had changed her. If she could change back.

He'd been paging through a soccer magazine that he'd bought for Paulo, unable to focus. He'd ask her about the letter right away. Why she'd kept it. What she knew. What she had been keeping from him all these years.

But when she finally walked in, bringing with her a burst of humid August air, Nuno couldn't say anything. He just listened as she groaned.

"It's too hot," she panted, dropping a sagging brown bag of groceries on the table before him. "Chicken for dinner." Nuno peered at her intently. Her forehead was damp with sweat, and some strands of graying hair were pasted to her face. She used to be beautiful, he thought. She was still pretty, though. Older-looking, but pretty. Was he still handsome? He could feel that his entire body had begun to shrink and droop with age over the last few years.

"I thought you were going to church?"

Helena checked the clock on the stove and then walked to the windowsill, where she kept her pills. He'd been surprised that there were so many, but they seemed to be working. After coming home that day and finding her all wrapped up in that business with the dog, Nuno just wanted her to get better. The doctor had made them go see another doctor together, a psychiatrist, and she called what had happened to Helena an "episode," prescribed a bunch of medication, and said that it would "take years to get to the heart of what caused it." The psychiatrist's office smelled like tobacco, and there were strange posters on the walls, of planets and pyramids. When they left, Nuno told Helena that they could handle their problems at home, together, without the woman who glared at him as if *he'd* done something wrong. What had he done? He'd convinced Mr. Costa not to go to the police and forgiven his wife for what she did. That was more than enough. He didn't need to sit in some woman's office and tell her how he felt about the whole goddamn thing.

Helena swallowed, sighed, and sat across from him. "I did. Short Mass. And then I go to pick up grocery."

Her English had improved, but she still screwed up a lot. Nuno didn't think she really cared about learning the language. Some days, he would correct her, but today he could only watch her silently. She picked up the soccer magazine, shrugged, and tossed it down. Then she smiled tiredly.

"What's the matter? You don't look good. You need to eat?" She kneaded her face with her hands. "I'll start soon, don't worry."

Nuno shook his head, finished his beer. "Where's Paulo?"

"He's running on the beach, Nuno, like you told him to."

"I don't think so."

Helena opened the refrigerator and peered inside.

"He should be running every day. He's not going to make it." Nuno waited as Helena nodded absently and moved her lips, talking to herself as she planned dinner. When she didn't respond, he left the room, wondering how much she really listened to him.

Paulo was quiet at the table, pushing bread into his mouth. His eyes were red.

"What were you doing at the beach?" Nuno asked.

"Running. Swimming."

"By yourself?"

"Yup."

"When do tryouts start?"

"You already asked me that, Dad," he said, his mouth full. His hair and his shirt were still wet.

"So?"

"Tomorrow."

"Well, what time?"

Paulo shrugged, signaling Helena to pass the butter dish. He mashed some onto his bread with a knife.

"Paulo, I need to know so I can bring you. There might be traffic."

"There's no traffic on Saturdays," he mumbled.

"Well, we should get there early, anyway."

"I don't want you to stay and watch," he said quickly, "and Chris can give me a ride home."

"Who's Chris?" asked Helena.

"He's trying out too. He's—"

"Not an athlete," Nuno snapped. Helena stared at him. He thought of her staring at Mateo, resting her head on his chest. "I will always re-member the first night," the letter had read. What had happened the first night? Nuno's stomach churned.

"Why don't you want me to watch?" he asked, trying to keep his voice calm. "My father always watched me, in Portugal, you know? He told me what to do to get better, he helped—"

"No, I don't want you to," said Paulo. He looked to Helena, but she pushed her food across her plate with her fork.

"Fine," Nuno said, "fine."

Paulo stared at him for a second. "Can I go?" he said.

"Where?" Helena asked.

"To watch TV," he said, standing and dumping his empty plate on the counter.

"Paulo, I made cookies," she called. "Paulo!"

Nuno and Helena sat there in the new emptiness, staring at each other. Nuno had always loved her eyes. They had faded, and the right eye was now the pale blue of the sky, while the left was a dull green. Nuno thought they were even more beautiful the way they were now.

Right then, Nuno wanted to tell her that he knew. That he'd always known. That he'd been there that night. That he'd watched her kneel down and begin to sob. "How could you?" she would whisper, and then her heavy steps would echo as she ran upstairs and slammed the door.

But Helena just sat there, drumming her fingers softly on the table. Nuno had noticed that since she'd been taking the medicine regularly, she'd been much more fidgety. She'd also started smoking more.

"Cigarette," she said as she walked toward the front door. "I clean after."

That night Nuno stayed downstairs and watched TV long after Paulo, and then Helena, went to bed. When Helena said goodnight to Paulo, she kissed his cheek and rubbed his back.

"Sleep well," she said in the way that she always did, starting low and ending on a high note. " 'Night, Dad," Paulo said as he went upstairs.

"Goodnight!" Nuno yelled loudly, and Helena looked over, scowling.

"I'm going up," she said. "Are you okay? You feel sick?"

He shook his head and watched as she slowly maneuvered out of the room. The blue lines of her veins climbed her calves.

Nuno could barely watch TV. Were they always this quiet around him? Something still felt off, and he couldn't put his finger on it. A beer might help, but he was tired and didn't feel like it.

It was warm out, and he walked out the front door and stood on the doorstep. It had been a good summer for the garden. Nuno had dug it out a bit and made it longer and wider this year, added some soil. In the shine of the moon he could see the cherry tomato plants weighed down with fruit. He inhaled the salt in the air and remembered Lagos. How different everything was. How, days after everything happened, Helena had come right up to him and touched her finger to his lower lip, where she'd cut him.

"I'm sorry," she had said.

"I'm sorry, too," he'd said. And that was that. Well, in some ways. She hadn't said one word about it since then, either. Not one word.

Nuno shut the door and climbed the stairs. It was a mistake. That's what Antonio called it in the days afterward, before he and Nuno stopped talking to each other altogether. A mistake.

The door to the bedroom was cracked open, but the room seemed darker than usual. Nuno searched for the light on the night table, knocking a book to the floor. Helena coughed and her eyes switched on.

When Nuno slid into bed, sleep wouldn't come. His finger lingered on his bottom lip. It had faded into a tiny mark, like a dimple. He remembered the way Helena swung her arm, the sudden taste of blood. His head spun and he rolled it across the pillow. His eyes clung to the crescent on the floor, the light from the hallway. It felt as though his life had become someone else's, but Nuno knew that wasn't true, it wasn't true at all. This life had always been his. He'd just chosen to ignore it.

Helena pressed against him, facing away. Nuno wanted, suddenly, to hold onto her as tightly as he could to stop the feeling that was washing over him, as if he was adrift in those waves again, being tossed by the current. It was out of his control, all of it. His heart drummed under the covers, and he yanked the covers down.

He rubbed his hands up and down Helena's legs. Eventually, she pulled him toward her. Her breath came long and easy now and her movements were slow, mechanical. Was she bored? Did she not want him anymore? Nuno tensed suddenly, and she reached back, feeling with her hand.

In the dim light, Nuno saw Mateo's face appear—the straight white gleam of his smile, the long locks of hair—and he knew that Helena had done this with him. That maybe she'd loved Mateo more than she could love him.

"What's the matter?" Helena whispered hesitantly.

Nuno rolled onto his back. His upper lip was wet.

"It's all right, dear," Helena said, rolling over. "It's all right. You must be getting sick." She was asleep within minutes.

—

Nuno awoke slowly and brought his knees up to his chest, waiting for his legs to brush Helena's. But they never did. He opened his eyes. The clock said nine.

"Where were you?" asked Paulo, glancing up from the table. Helena placed a mug of steaming coffee in front of Nuno as he sat down.

"There are more pancakes," she said over her shoulder. "We were waiting."

Paulo gulped his juice. "Are you sick? It's so late."

"Why didn't you wake me?" Nuno asked Helena groggily.

"Maybe you needed it," she said, coming over and putting a hand on his shoulder. "Your body needed it. You feel better?"

Nuno could smell the grease on her oven mitt. "Sure," he said. Paulo stood up. The shirt he was wearing said "The Beatles" in faded lettering. "Where did you get that?"

"What?"

"That shirt."

"I've had this for a year. What time are we leaving?"

Nuno stared at him. Tryouts. "We're leaving at ten."

"That's in a half hour!"

"Right. Get ready."

Paulo dragged his way upstairs.

"Did he say something?"

"I didn't hear anything." Helena piled pancakes on his plate and filled his coffee cup to the brim, so that it would be impossible to lift without spilling.

"Nuno, it happen to everyone. Never happen before, right? Maybe just one time, that's it. *Não se preocupe.*"

Nuno sat there and stared ahead, past the bottles of pills on the windowsill, out to where the sun was shining. Helena was cleaning up, whistling to herself. She paused and followed his gaze.

"Better get those tomatoes soon," she warned. "Ripe. Ready to burst."

There was no traffic as they drove to the field.

"We're going to be there so early," said Paulo, rolling down his window. "Can you open your window?"

"You want to be there early," Nuno said, cranking it down, "so the coach knows you care. Trust me, now. Is it still Coach—"

"Davis? Yeah."

"Ah, you need a Portuguese coach. Davis doesn't know what he's doing."

"He's fine."

"You nervous?"

Paulo didn't say anything, just looked out the window. Nuno saw he had his fist clenched in his lap.

"It's okay to be nervous, Paulo. I used to get—"

"I'm fine, Dad," he said, as they pulled down the dirt road to the soccer fields.

"Thanks," he said, jumping out.

Nuno watched the other boys on the field. No one really looked at Paulo. They were all standing around, talking, laughing with one another. A few of them were kicking the ball around. Nuno wished someone would call out to his son. He had a friend or two here, right?

"Okay," said Paulo, putting his bag over his shoulder and backing away.

"Well, maybe I'll stay for a bit," Nuno said.

"There's no other parents here," Paulo said over his shoulder as he walked away, "and Mom promised you wouldn't. Please don't, all right? Please?"

Nuno put the car in drive and pulled away.

⌒

It was almost eleven. There wouldn't be a game on at the Lusitania Club until at least one, and that was if he was lucky.

It was dark in the club and the TV was bright. Soccer highlights were on—Portugal in the 1966 World Cup semifinal against England nine years ago. They'd lost. Nuno took his favorite stool, and Luis walked over, holding the newspaper.

"Early!" he said. "Sporting isn't on 'til one today."

Nuno shrugged and forced a grin. "How about red?"

He drank gratefully, gazing at the television. Luis walked over and leaned against the bar. "How's Paulo?"

"At tryouts."

"And Helena?"

"Doing good. How's Kim?"

Luis cleared his throat. "She's okay."

Nuno nodded. His wine was nearly gone. Luis was staring at him blankly. Nuno glanced away from him. The night that it had happened, he'd gone to the club to watch Sporting in the UEFA Cup. Luis hadn't been there, and everyone was drunk, including Kim, who was bartending. After she closed, she led him out to the parking lot, where they started kissing, huddled together in the darkness.

"Let's go somewhere," he'd said. They'd ended up at a crappy hotel on a bed with stained sheets, both sneaking home after a few hours to lie about where they'd been.

He noticed how tired Luis looked. "The thing is, Nuno," he said, "Kim ain't doing so well."

Suddenly Nuno remembered the way Kim's hair smelled like dark rum that night, the way it fell across his face.

"What's wrong?"

Luis stared at the clock above the bar and sighed. "She got cancer."

"Shit. I'm sorry."

Nuno's face felt itchy and hot. Once he'd realized, after it happened, that Kim wasn't going to tell Luis, he'd been able to relax a little. He still felt terrible. But it was only that one time, and he was drunk. Kim got a job at another bar, and he never saw her anymore. Things happened. He couldn't go back and fix it.

"More wine?"

Nuno nodded. The phone rang in the back room, and Luis put the bottle down next to his glass and walked away.

⌒

That night Nuno lay in bed, motionless. During the game, a bunch of guys had come in and they'd stayed out afterward, drinking wine, bullshitting. Dinner had passed by blurrily. Paulo had said he was tired from tryouts and gone to bed early, and there was nothing on TV.

Helena spat into the sink in the bathroom and hummed to herself. Nuno wondered if she was upset about the night before. Maybe she was right, it was a one-time thing. It happened to everyone. She'd acted normal at dinner, but a few times he'd caught her looking at him oddly.

The important thing was to stop thinking about it. But the thought of trying again didn't excite him like it usually did. It actually made him nervous.

Nuno put his magazine down as she turned off the light on her side. They lay there, not touching. Was she waiting for him, or was she hoping that he didn't try anything? For a second, Nuno wanted to just walk away. There were three beers left in the fridge. He could sit at the table and wait until she fell asleep, and then tell her he'd been sick.

But then he felt Helena's breath on his shoulder.

"Sorry," he said, "I'm not—"

"Shhhh," she whispered, "stop. Let me help you."

In a few seconds her mouth was on him. As he reached down to pull her up, because he knew it was no use, Kim flashed into Nuno's mind. She was bending over the bed, her face turned away.

It felt good. Helena hadn't done this in years. He didn't deserve it. He thought of Mateo, wondered with a hazy start if she'd done this to him, but suddenly it didn't matter. His hand sank into the back of her hair. The darkness was soft and warm and smooth.

"I love you," Nuno said quietly, when they were finished.

But Helena didn't hear him. She was already asleep.

—

Four days later, Nuno was at the club when he decided that it was time to confront Helena. It wasn't just that he kept imagining her with Mateo It was the idea that she could go on forever not knowing that he *knew*.

"How's Kim?" he asked Luis as he stood up to leave.

Luis shook his head and held up his hand.

Walking into the house, Nuno felt a little unsteady. He wondered where Paulo was. He didn't like him hanging out with Chris; the kid's parents were hippies and Chris had long hair, wore sunglasses, and was a horrible soccer player. Nuno had seen him tripping all over the place at tryouts last year.

He wasn't sure why he'd gotten drunk again. Maybe it was being around Luis lately, the way he avoided Nuno's eyes as he filled his glass. He didn't look as though he'd been sleeping, and he drifted around the bar in a haze.

When Helena walked in, Nuno was staring out the window and watching the rain. She glared at him, dropped the bag on the counter, then peered back outside.

"C'mon, honey," she said loudly. "Don't get wet. Get inside." She whispered something softly in Portuguese that Nuno couldn't make out.

"I'm coming," Paulo said, walking sheepishly. He was soaked, holding his socks and shin guards up against his chest. Helena felt how wet his back was and grimaced. "Go shower, you'll get sick," she ordered.

Paulo nodded and ventured a look at Nuno.

"Well? What happened?"

Helena noisily unloaded the bag of groceries onto the table.

"Did you find out?" Nuno asked, standing and extending his arms.

"Yeah," Paulo said. "I didn't make it."

"Shit!" Nuno slammed his hand on the table. "That fucking guy doesn't know what he's talking about! Coach Davis—"

"It's okay, Dad," called Paulo, escaping upstairs. "It's cool."

"No it's not!" Nuno's voice was louder than he wanted. "It's not okay! That's the problem with you! *It's not okay!* If you even *cared* about it you'd know—"

"It's okay, Nuno," said Helena, stepping in front of him. Her jaw was set and her nostrils flared.

The bathroom door slammed and the shower squeaked on.

"It's okay," she said, nodding, her hands on her hips. "There's next year, right? *Vai dar tudo certo.*"

Nuno crossed his arms and glared at her. This was it. He'd tell her that he knew about Mateo. That he knew that she'd never truly loved him.

"Helena, listen."

She looked back at him defiantly, her eyebrows raised. Now was the time.

But he couldn't.

"*Certo,*" Nuno said finally, quietly, and sat back down.

The fire in Helena's eyes dimmed. She nodded and walked over to the stove.

Nuno knew at that moment that everything would keep going exactly as it had been in the past. He could almost see the way his life would play out, the way all of their lives would.

And he knew that he would never tell Helena what he'd done.

It was simple. She just didn't need to know.

plastic chairs

CATARINA · 2008

Catarina and Shannon sat outside of a café on Gran Via. The glossy tablecloth rippled in the wind, and the crescent moon looked as though it was made of the same white paper and fastened to the clouds.

Their husbands, Max and Walter, were in their beds back in the hotel, in rooms 102 and 103.

"Cat," Shannon said. "I bought cigarettes." She tapped her pocketbook. "Like we talked about?'

Catarina shook her head and stared at Shannon's red, sunburned chest. Her dress was cut low, and her breasts threatened to spill out. Catarina had worn the tight dress that Shannon had convinced her to wear, but compared to Shannon she felt plain and boring. "We didn't talk about anything. You just said you wanted to start smoking again."

"You should try one. Are you going to try one?"

"No," Catarina said, "I won't." The thought of it made her feel ill. She could see the black smoke coursing down her throat and soaking like ink into her pink lungs. "People spend years trying to quit smoking. Doesn't it seem strange to you to want to start over?"

Shannon pursed her lips and drew the pack of cigarettes from an inner pocket of her purse. She slid her hand carefully under the plastic wrap, then pricked it with the fingernail of her index finger. It peeled back and came off all in one piece. "It's not strange," she said, examining the box. Health warnings were printed in Spanish over graphic pictures. CUIDADO, this one said. IMPOTENCIA. It had a tiny picture of a man and a woman sitting in bed. The man looked sad, the woman angry. Shannon snickered and held the pack up, but Catarina looked away.

The street was quiet. They'd met, as planned, at the café on the corner. One block away loomed their hotel, a bulky white building framed by palm trees with gray, peeling bark. To their right, in the corner, a man who looked to be in his forties was sitting across from a young girl.

Shannon drummed the pack against her palm. "We have to order something."

"Get a drink," said Catarina.

"What are you having?"

"A bottle of water."

Shannon rolled her eyes, shrugged, and motioned for the waiter. He had a damp white towel slung over his shoulder, and there was a smudge of something black on his arm. She ordered in broken Spanish that was strung together loosely with false bursts of laughter.

Catarina suddenly felt very tired. She envisioned peeling back the covers to the bed, sliding onto the taut white sheets that looked soft but felt like cardboard. She'd sleep as late as she pleased. She'd trained Max not to touch her when he awoke, no matter how badly he wanted to.

"We should both be drinking," Shannon said.

"I'm tired," said Catarina. "And there's no one here, Shannon."

"Who did you expect to be here?"

"Well, someone."

Shannon pointed at the man seated in the corner. The girl was now leaning close to him, the plastic chair under her bending. The man cradled her face in his hands.

"I bet that's not his daughter," Shannon said loudly, raising one eyebrow.

The girl had bare feet and wore a red handkerchief in her hair. Catarina wondered what it felt like to have those big, heavy fingers pressed against her temples.

Shannon downed half of her glass of sangria and motioned for another. Catarina took a sip of water and kicked off her sandals under the table.

"Jesus, have a fucking drink." Shannon's voice became more desperate.

Catarina shrugged and motioned to the waiter, her fingers snapping across the blank sky. There was really no reason not to. Besides, just being around Shannon lately put her on edge. If she brought up what she wanted to, she risked an argument, and she didn't care enough about it to get into a full-blown fight. Or did she? A piece of her wondered if Shannon had betrayed her, but it was a small piece. Betrayal, she thought, was human. Lying and even cheating were a bigger part of all of their lives than they chose to admit.

The waiter smiled skeptically when he brought her sangria. Headlights sparked in the street behind them.

"That's my girl," said Shannon. She rolled a cigarette between her fingers and then lit it with a snap. "Let's get out of here," she said, holding the smoke in. "The bar over there looks much better." She gestured to the place across the street, where a crowd of people streamed from a beat-up taxi. "Let's do something that isn't on the goddamn itinerary."

Catarina thought of the crisp white copies that Max had printed before they left. They read "Madrid, 2008" across the top, and "Free Time" was even a category. That was just the way that Max was. He'd never seemed to consider exactly *why* she'd married him, or if he had, he'd never mentioned it. Had he ever wondered if it was just for his money? Catarina had no way of knowing. There had always been men who desired her; some were better looking, a few had even been wealthier, but in the beginning, Catarina used to like how much her mere presence pleased Max. There was an honest simplicity in his infatuation with her that she envied, because she could never feel that way.

Over the past six months, though, things had changed, and Catarina had stopped having sex with him altogether. At night, she pretended to sleep while he lay next to her, waiting anxiously. It saddened Catarina a little, because she thought that Max was a decent man at heart. But recently, she wondered about Shannon. She knew that her friend had come over to see Max when she wasn't there. She knew that Shannon didn't give a shit about Walter. It was impossible, lately, to not question everything.

"Cat? Let's go. *Vamos!*" Shannon said. Catarina couldn't help but admire the way she exhaled a perfect ring of silver.

On the patio next door, women in bright red dresses and sandals flashed yellow smiles at men with slicked-back hair. Candle flames shivered in the wind as cars rattled the street.

"This is perfect," breathed Shannon, grabbing Catarina by the back of her shirt as they walked by the bouncer.

"Sangria," shouted Catarina to the bartender. His hair was gray and he wore a wrinkled tuxedo. Shannon reached out and yanked at his bow tie.

"*Señorita,*" he said, "*porfavor, Señorita.*"

Laughter erupted from two men at the side of the bar. Catarina thought they looked too young to even be there. One of them wore a ponytail, and the other's head was shaved. The one with the ponytail grinned at her. She pretended not to notice.

At the table, Shannon drank quickly and nodded her head to the music, but her movements were off-rhythm. The hostess appeared before them in a yellow dress. Catarina could smell her perfume.

"There will be a flamenco show inside in fifteen minutes," the girl whispered, as if telling a secret. She went on to the next table.

Shannon lit another cigarette. "What did she say?"

"Flamenco," Catarina said. Her head was beginning to feel light. She was happier. There would be time to talk later. She wasn't sure she had ever truly loved Max. Maybe Shannon had just made a mistake. Maybe nothing had happened. Really, did any of it matter? Catarina felt as if she could just float away. There was no way to stop time, no way to go back. But what if she could figure out a way to forget everything? What if she could render herself blank, and become someone else? Perhaps all of her decisions since leaving Portugal had been wrong. Perhaps there was still time to change them.

Shannon and Catarina walked inside, where the dark room smelled of stale beer and music pounded incessantly. They stood near the bar and watched a man ready the small stage, moving chairs around and setting up a microphone.

Shannon pulled Catarina onto the dance floor and began to swing her around awkwardly. Some of the men who were standing against the wall whistled. One of them suddenly squeezed his wiry body in between them, taking each of their hands and twirling them. He was short and had a toothpick clenched in his mouth. His hand slipped down Catarina's arm, darted into her armpit for a second, and then wrapped tightly around her waist. Catarina recoiled and pushed hard against his bony ribs.

"Pervert," Shannon muttered, pulling her away. "I think the show is starting. Look."

She pointed to the stage just as the music from the stereo was abruptly shut off. Two women in white ruffled dresses appeared, and they were joined by two men with guitars. One of the men spoke into the microphone but his voice was drowned out by a squeal of feedback.

"Let's go back outside," said Shannon.

"Why?"

"Didn't you see those guys at the bar? Looking at us?"

The music began. The women stamped their feet, the thick soles of their shoes drumming the wooden stage. The plucking of guitars intertwined and the strings rang as the beat grew faster. The sequins on the women's dresses glinted.

Shannon bobbed her head. Catarina saw again that she was hopelessly off-rhythm.

"Those guys looked fifteen, Shannon," said Catarina as she followed her through the door.

Outside, a crowd had gathered, and everyone was pressed against the bar, their voices echoing in the damp air. Catarina could only understand Spanish if people spoke slowly and directly to her. Many of the words and sounds were similar to Portuguese, but she didn't find it nearly as beautiful.

"They're still here," said Shannon, pointing to the bar.

"I think I see a table in the corner," said Catarina. "I'm going to sit down."

From the table she watched Shannon slide in between the guy with the ponytail and his friend. Soon they were all nodding and staring back at her, and she wished she had a cigarette, or a drink, something to hold.

"They bought us drinks," Shannon said when they followed her over to the table, "and they speak English."

"Where are the chairs?" asked the guy with the shaved head.

"Go get some," said the other. "From inside."

"I'll sit with her," said Shannon, and perched on Catarina's lap. Inside they could hear the music reaching a frenzied pitch. People were cheering and shouting along with the stamping and the furious twang of the guitars.

Shannon lit a cigarette and coughed. "Oh, it's good, Cat," she wheezed, "so good to be back."

The guy with the ponytail stood awkwardly before them, bouncing back and forth from one foot to the other.

"Your friend didn't tell me your name," he said to Catarina.

Catarina shrugged. "How old are you?"

"Her name's Catarina," Shannon said.

"I'm Diego," he said, sitting down, "and this is Francisco."

"You didn't answer my question," said Catarina.

"Cat, don't be a bitch," said Shannon.

"That's all right," said Diego. "I'm twenty, and Francisco is twenty-two."

"Are you lying?" asked Catarina. Shannon blew smoke into the air. Diego pulled his chair closer to her. "Yes," he said, laughing, "I'm nineteen."

Francisco pushed closer to Shannon and put his hand on her back. "I bet you're around my age," he said, and she leaned her head on his shoulder for a second.

"You don't sound American," Diego said, staring at Catarina intently.

"*Eu sou Português*," she said. She liked the way his T-shirt clung to his arms. He was talking to her very carefully, as if he knew that if he said one thing wrong, she'd walk away. It was almost amusing.

Shannon lit Francisco's cigarette with the tip of hers and touched his bicep with her hand. "Nice," she said as he flexed proudly, "very nice."

She might as well just start taking her clothes off, Catarina thought. But this had been the plan, hadn't it? Even if they'd never said it, isn't this what they'd both been driving at? Isn't this why they'd gone out without their husbands?

"Let's go inside and dance," said Diego.

"Catarina is a fabulous dancer," said Shannon.

"More sangria, Catarina?" asked Diego.

"Thank you," she said, smiling at him. He overfilled her glass, and sangria pooled on the table and dribbled into her lap.

"You idiot!" said Francisco.

"It's okay," said Catarina, blotting at her white skirt with her napkin. The stain was right on her crotch. It looked like blood. She could feel Diego staring at it.

"That might stain, Cat. You should go to the bathroom and get some soap," warned Shannon.

"Fucking idiot," said Francisco.

Catarina looked at the red blotches. "It'll be fine."

Diego looked horrified. He kept extending his hand toward her lap and then pulling it back. "I'm sorry," he said again. "I'll go get some soap. What can I do? What should I do?"

"No," Catarina said, "that's all right. It's just kind of cold. See?" She put her hand on his and brought it into her lap and his eyes widened. His open palm was warm as she pressed it down.

When the four of them went back inside, Catarina mostly watched Shannon, how easily she rubbed her body against Francisco. Diego was bolder now, and he rubbed her back as they bobbed their heads, crushed against each other by the crowd, their words drowned out by the crescendo of voices. He put his arm around her as Catarina danced, but she shook it off. She liked the feeling of disappearing into the crowd, and once she pushed away from all of them, feeling the heat and the noise as it threatened to swallow her. When she found her way back through the crowd, Diego grinned.

"Thought you left me," he said.

Finally, Shannon put a sweaty arm around Catarina and pulled her neck roughly. Their heads banged into each other's.

"We can go to Francisco's," said Shannon. "I'm going to Francisco's."

Catarina nodded. "What do we tell our husbands?" she said.

"Good question. We'll tell them that you drank too much and got sick, and we slept on the beach together."

Catarina looked at her friend's drooping eyes, the lines etched in her forehead that she covered with makeup. She felt far away from her already. Far away from Max. Far from everyone.

Diego put his arm around her waist. "Let's go," he said.

Francisco lived in a small apartment a few blocks away, near the Plaza de Espana. He poured them each a glass of red wine and shoved magazines and dirty paper plates off the couch so they could sit down. Diego put on a CD and sat next to Catarina on the couch as Shannon and Francisco danced, gripping each other as if they each feared that this could all disappear at any moment. Diego slipped his hand inside Catarina's shirt and his fingers traced up her spine. When the song ended, Francisco led Shannon into the kitchen, and then a door slammed and Catarina flinched.

It had happened even faster than Catarina expected. Even Diego's hand stopped moving and just hovered there. Catarina stood to look at a picture on the wall. It was a blown-up photograph of green mountains speckled with white churches and pink houses. In the distance, atop the mountains, there was what looked like an enormous palace.

"Where is that?" Catarina asked.

"Granada. I have family there."

"It looks nice."

"It's beautiful there. That is the Alhambra. We can go there someday. Come back over here."

Catarina walked to the window and looked out. Below them, the crowded lights of the city shone yellow and white. Brake lights blinked on in warning, and then disappeared.

"Come back," Diego said again.

When she sat back down, Diego immediately kissed her neck, her ears, the sides of her face. Catarina let him take off her shirt and touch her breasts.

"It's still wet," he said, running his hand over the red stain on her skirt. But his hands felt colder now. The CD blared as Diego pressed her back into the couch. His face was so eager that she almost wanted to. But when he reached to yank down her skirt she shook her head, and his hands paused, trembling against her stomach.

"No, not tonight," she said simply.

Diego's face rippled in amazement. His mouth jutted open. "What?"

"I don't want to." She could feel how hard he was, pressed against her. The music grew louder.

"You don't—you don't? Then what are we doing here? Why are we here?" Diego leaned down on her with all his weight, bouncing on top of her. "That's not fair," he said frantically. "Come on!"

Catarina waited a moment, let him get comfortable again, let him kiss her neck, and then elbowed him in the side as hard as she could. "Off!" she said loudly, rolling out from under him.

"What's wrong with you?!" He looked as though he might stand up and grab her, but he punched the couch cushion and then slumped on his stomach. *"Puta!"*

Catarina's head was spinning. She looked down at Diego. "Calm down," she said. "It's not your fault. I'm sure you're very good." But he was probably too young, too inexperienced. In the same way that Max was too old and predictable.

"I am!" he said, sitting up hopefully. "Look, just give me a chance." He lowered his voice. "I'm sorry, okay? Give me the chance."

"I can't," she said, shrugging. But as she turned, he stood up and grabbed her waist. He held onto her with such wiry strength that for a second she was worried, and she froze there, locked together with this man she didn't know. This child.

The song ended. Diego's fingers dug into her back. Catarina didn't move. Suddenly, they could both hear Shannon moaning in the other room.

Diego relaxed his grip, breathing heavily, then let go. Catarina stumbled forward. Diego looked embarrassed and collapsed on the couch, pouring more wine. "I'm sorry," he kept saying. "I didn't mean anything by it. You're just so beautiful. I am sorry, I am."

Out on the street pigeons squatted silently, waiting for dawn.

~

"My head hurts," announced Shannon. "Did you fuck him?"

"Jesus, Shannon."

"Well, did you?"

"No. Did you?"

Shannon stumbled in her heels and leaned against Catarina, resting her head on her shoulder. "Yeah. And it was pretty good, too. Younger men don't get tired, you know?"

Catarina thought of Diego's pleading face, how he'd written his number on a napkin and made her take it.

"Why didn't you?" asked Shannon. "Cat?"

Catarina ignored her. The sky was growing brighter.

"Have you ever slept with Max, Shannon?"

"What?"

"Just tell me."

Shannon stared at Catarina. "What are you talking about? Of course not!" Shannon's teeth and lips were stained red with wine. "What, just because of tonight?"

Catarina knew that Shannon was lying. She'd have bet her life on it. In one movement she twisted away from Shannon's grasp and bent her arm behind her. Catarina felt Shannon exhale sharply in surprise and pain, and then go silent. The street was impossibly quiet. Shannon was trembling.

"Forget it," Catarina said, letting go. "I must still be drunk. Forget it."

Shannon kneeled down and clutched her stomach. "How can I *forget* it? Where did you—why did you—"

"Let's just forget this whole night."

"No, Cat, I can't. I *loved* this night. I loved getting you out here, getting you to, I don't know, open *up* a little, you know?" She sat on the curb and put her head between her legs, groaning. Catarina could see her underwear.

"You know that's what people say, right, about you?" Shannon's voice was hoarse.

"What do they say? What does who say?"

Shannon spat. "You're closed off. You are. And I just wanted to—"

"Did Max say that, Shannon?" Catarina was growing impatient. She had to pee. Dawn was crawling in, and it would bring the heat of the sun and the hustle of the locals to the street. "Shannon, get up."

"I'm going to be sick." Shannon's head bobbed woozily. "What the hell is wrong with you? I mean, really, you're—"

"I just want someone—anyone—to tell me the goddamn truth. Everything, *everything* lately has been so . . ."

Catarina heard her words echo, watched them disappear into the white light of morning. Then she turned and began to walk away. "It doesn't matter." She heard the warm slap of vomit hitting the pavement, but she didn't look back.

Slipping into the cool, abandoned lobby, Catarina thought of how it had felt to twist Shannon's arm. She could've broken it easily. How would it feel to snap thin bones, to tear muscle? What would have happened if she hadn't let go?

That was the thing. There was no one to answer to anymore. And she wasn't going to let herself go back to Lisbon, to aunts and uncles who would say things like "We've been expecting you," to her cousin Rui, who would embrace her and then hold her at arm's length, smirking, examining her face.

⌒

Catarina had been careful not to wake Max. She took only two of his four credit cards and all of the cash from his wallet, and left a note on the table. It read: *Please do not look for me. I do not love you. I'm going away.*

The air smelled of coffee and plantains. Stray cats yawned and licked in the stubby, burnt-out bushes along the sides of the street. Catarina bought a bottle of water and an orange at a small café. There were flowers in small wooden boxes at each table, the colors shockingly bright. The woman behind the counter held a child in her arms. Behind her a small dog, his white fur tinged with red dirt, slept in the shadows.

Catarina pointed to the baby. *"¿Su nombre?"* she asked hesitantly.

"Miguel," the woman said, proudly rocking her son. Her face was blotchy and craggy and dark hair hung limply to her shoulders. *"?Y tu?"*

"Catarina."

The woman smiled at her. *"¿Es usted Español?"*

"No, eu sou Portuguesa," said Catarina. *"¿Puedo?"*

Catarina reached over the cash register. The baby was heavier than she'd thought. He pushed at her chest restlessly with a chubby foot.

Catarina turned and looked through the window, holding Miguel tightly. A bus rolled slowly into view and came to a stop. "Where does that one go?" she asked.

"Granada," said the woman, touching Catarina's back with her hand and pointing. *"Si, Granada. Muy hermoso."*

The bus sighed in the heat. The two women stared at it silently. Miguel opened his eyes and began to cry.

"Give back." The woman held out her arms. "Give back. He cry *todo el dia*. Give back."

Catarina handed Miguel back to his mother and watched her rock him until he quieted down. Then, in the new silence, both women fixed their eyes on the window, each of them waiting for something.

the dog

Helena had considered poisoning his food. Well, maybe she hadn't *considered* it, but she'd allowed herself to imagine it. Sometimes, while serving dinner, as Nuno just sat there with his arms outstretched on the table, she imagined him clutching at his chest, his face wrinkling in shock. He would cry out for help, but she would just stand there, watching, until his head slumped on the table.

She would never do anything like this, of course. Because of Paulo. And because she couldn't. Helena was fairly certain that one horrible thing happened to each person in their lifetime. Hers had occurred when she was nineteen, and if she was being honest with herself, she'd lied about it ever since. That's why she felt so trapped sometimes, but that was also why she'd made no real effort to change anything. If it wasn't for Paulo, things might've been different. She'd had two miscarriages before him, and after the second they'd both thought that was it. Maybe they weren't meant to have a child. Helena remembered how empty she felt, lying in bed with her hands clasped over her deflated stomach. Staring at the pile of white towels stained with blood on the floor.

Then they'd had Paulo, surprising both of them, and the doctor had recommended that they stop there. He didn't think her body could take anymore. Not that they could afford another child, anyway. When they first arrived in the States, Helena had worked in the same auto-parts factory as Nuno, standing on the assembly line with the other women in that huge garage that smelled of oil and stale deodorant. She could feel Nuno's eyes on her even when he wasn't there, and she rarely talked to the other women, and didn't even look at the other men.

When she did pray, easing onto her already arthritic knees, all alone in the pew because Nuno had stopped going to Mass years before, she prayed for Nuno first, and herself last. But she prayed for herself the longest. She *wouldn't* poison his food. Most of the time, she couldn't even believe that those thoughts crept in. Helena was forty-three years old, and she had the feeling that she could live for another forty years. She just needed to figure out the best *way* to live. She tried to be the American housewife that Nuno wanted, but to be honest, she never really felt like herself. She tried to be thankful that she didn't need to work in the factory anymore as she cooked, cleaned, and mothered her way through each day, then gave herself willingly to Nuno at night, if he was in the mood. But sometimes she missed the yelping pulleys, the nonstop roll of the rubber belts, the whine and grind of machinery. At least in the factory, with her goggles fogging up, her tongue scalded by hot coffee, she knew she was alive.

Now, the only time she really felt she was *there* was with Paulo. Helena knew that he was a gentle soul; she could tell by the look in his eyes. She hoped that she and Nuno were doing a good job raising him. She was trying as hard as she could, she knew that. It was harder than she thought, though, definitely harder than she thought.

On her knees in the dim church, she squinted as she did at Igreja de Santo António in Lagos when she was a girl, so that the candle flames at the altar flickered violently. She tried to imagine that Deus himself was telling her how to live out the rest of her life. She tried to listen. But she was never quite sure what He would say.

Yesterday was when Helena first saw the dog. She was cooking breakfast when it came rooting through the garden behind the house. It was late spring in Narragansett, and as the rains and warmer days came, Nuno spent hours planting and weeding the garden, a cigar dangling from his mouth. Helena remembered the day that Nuno had bought the house, paying ten thousand dollars in damp cash. They'd stood out on the lawn together, and he'd told her proudly that it had been his dream to have a garden. "But," Helena said, "in Lagos my father had acres of gardens, with all the fruit and vegetables that you could want."

"This isn't Lagos," he told her, tapping her nose with his index finger, shaking his head as if she were a silly young girl. "This is better than Lagos."

The garden was important to Nuno. Helena knew that. And Paulo, who was five years old now, loved it out there. *"Cuidado, Paulo, cuidado!"* called Nuno when their son ran recklessly through the rows of plants chasing a ball. So when Helena saw a dog trampling through things with muddy paws, she rapped on the windowpane. "Get out!" she cried.

The dog paid her no mind. It was black, short-haired, and muscular, with a trace of white in its long tail. Helena's hands were covered in egg yolk and some of it splashed on the window, but this was important! It was Nuno's garden! She knocked again. *"Sai!* Out!" But the dog dug his head down and sniffed, wagging his tail.

"Mom?" Paulo was standing behind her in his pajamas, looking up at the yellow egg sliding down the window.

"Sit and eat, hon," Helena said, searching for the dog. He must've finally heard her, because he was nowhere to be seen. She breathed a sigh of relief. When she turned back to the table, there was Nuno in his bathrobe, staring at her angrily and wiping sleep from his eyes.

"What's wrong with you?" he asked. "What'd you do?"

Helena told him about the black dog in the garden.

"I've never seen him," he said, peering out the window. "The only people around here with a dog are the Costas. And Riley's white, not black."

"A stray dog? Stray?" she said, placing bacon and pancakes on his plate.

Nuno picked up one of the pancakes, stared closely at it, and then threw it back on his plate.

"What happened to these? They look different."

Helena hadn't done anything different with the pancakes. She didn't know what he was talking about. But she made him some more, because she didn't feel like getting into anything.

Finally Nuno pushed his plate away and ran a hand over his mouth. "I'll take Paulo to school on my way to work, since you woke me up so early, banging on the damn window."

"I'm sorry," she said, "but it was the dog. Not me."

"Paulo," Nuno called out, "We're leaving for school in ten minutes."

Before they left, Paulo ran over and sat on Helena's lap. "I don't want to go," he said, the thumb in his mouth making his words muffled. "I wanna stay with you."

Nuno stood in the doorway, buttoning his shirt. "*Jesus Cristo*, don't baby him!" He turned to Paulo. "Let's go."

Paulo clutched at Helena and nuzzled her face until Nuno came over and heaved him over his shoulder. Helena thought Paulo would scream, but he just hung there silently,

Nuno patted him on the back and grabbed his keys from the counter. "What's for dinner tonight?" he asked as he stepped outside.

"What you want?" she called, but the door shut and a minute later she heard his car stutter on.

Helena spent the morning doing laundry and cleaning the bedroom. She didn't really clean Nuno's side of the room anymore, because of the stuff she used to find in his bureau. First it was just magazines, and that really didn't bother her. They started out relatively clean—lingerie catalogs that she'd thought she'd discarded, sports magazine swimsuit issues—but soon it was worse stuff, like *Playboy*. Maybe she shouldn't have opened the drawers, but she was just putting his socks and underwear away. Once she knew they were in there, though, she couldn't *not* open the drawers. In those pages, the women looked cheap, with their heavy makeup, and so skinny! Was this what Nuno wanted, Helena wondered? Then why had he ended up with her?

If that was where it had stayed, with the magazines, then it would have been easier. But Helena knew things that Nuno didn't think she knew. Years ago, right in the middle of one of the magazines, where the pages folded out, she'd found a different type of picture. It was a photograph of a woman who had signed the back in cursive. At first, she'd nearly convinced herself that it was the kind of picture Nuno could have bought somewhere. But then, a few weeks later, she stopped into the Lusitania Club to see her husband. She rarely went there, but she'd seen his car out front and had gone in to see when he was coming home for dinner.

Nuno was sitting at the bar talking to the bartender, and he didn't even turn around when Helena came in. She sat down next to him and was hit with a wave of perfume; the same scent she'd noticed on his neck one recent night, mixing with his aftershave. Helena didn't say anything, and she left soon after, floating back out to the car. The gray clouds pressed down on her, the cool air clogged her throat when she tried to swallow.

She stopped looking for other photos and stopped cleaning anything on his side of the room, letting dust gather on the far window and clothes and papers pile on the floor. She knew he'd noticed that something had changed. But she didn't waste time feeling bad for herself, because she also felt that it was probably what she deserved. She knew that Deus had a plan for her, and that a lot of what had happened to her, and to Nuno, was her fault. The thing was, she didn't used to think about all of it so much—things she could've done differently, things she maybe shouldn't have done at all. But lately, she couldn't get the nagging thoughts out of her head. Sometimes, it felt like a dull whine that she couldn't turn off. At its loudest, it was a cloud of angry bees, swarming and buzzing right next to her temples.

It was early afternoon. As Helena scrubbed the dishes, half of her mind was on planning dinner. But the other half was on that damn dog. She almost *wanted* him to come back so that Nuno would believe her. She'd seen it with her own eyes! Paulo had too, she thought, though she wasn't sure.

With all of her chores done, Helena strolled outside and ended up in the garden, wandering about. It wasn't long before she saw them. In the wet, dewy earth where Nuno had just planted tomato seeds and carefully raked the soil were small paw prints.

Helena bent down to inspect them, and then grinned. She felt justified. But wait a second! Some of the older tomato plants had even been trampled and chewed! Nuno was *not* going to like this! He'd been out for hours last Sunday tending to the garden. But the dog didn't care about that, and he didn't care about them. Helena circled the garden and then the house, searching for more evidence, her head swimming. She could see Nuno's outraged face when she showed him. It wasn't right. It just wasn't right.

Right then, standing on the lawn, hands on her hips, she resolved to catch the dog. It would be something that would take work, but she didn't mind. It was something for her to do. And it was something that

Nuno would *want* her to do. It would be for him. Well, it would be for both of them.

In Paulo's room Helena found some construction paper and a small bucket of colored pencils, mostly dull or chewed. She chose a piece of yellow paper and found a blue pencil and went back to the kitchen, where she filled the tea kettle and sat down at the kitchen table, pulling the curtains apart so that she could see the garden.

She wrote: ANSWERS.

Then under it she wrote: THE DOG.

She already felt as though she were getting somewhere. When she lifted the shiny kettle, her blurry face smiled proudly back. She couldn't see the lines under her eyes or her graying hair. Instead, she saw someone who was taking control, who was getting things done. She poured her tea, keeping one eye on the window, and then sat down to write: IDEAS.

The phone began ringing, but she decided that this was more important and that it was probably for Nuno, anyway. She came up with three ideas right away, though she wasn't sure she should write the third one down.

I. SAVE THE GARDEN

2. CATCH THE DOG

3.

It looked strange, though, to have the number three just sitting there by itself, so she erased it. She'd keep her last idea inside for now.

By the time Nuno came home at half past five, Helena was making dinner. She'd almost sliced her finger on the cutting board as she tried to pay attention to the garden at all times.

"Helena?" Nuno yelled as he slapped the newspaper against the counter. "Honestly, what's wrong with you?"

Paulo ran in and buried his head in her waist. He was sniffling.

"What happen?" she asked, holding onto Paulo and turning so that she could still see out the window.

"Um, you were supposed to pick him up?" said Nuno incredulously. "His teacher called me from school! Ms. Sanderson. She brought him to my work. He was the last one there! What happened to you?"

"Oh, *desculpe,*" she murmured, stroking Paulo's face as Nuno paced behind them. "I was busy." She remembered the phone ringing repeatedly in the empty house.

Paulo stopped sniffling. "I'm hungry," he said. "Can I go outside until supper time?"

"Yes," Helena said, "but not in the garden."

He didn't ask why.

"What were you doing that you were so fucking busy?" Nuno waited until Paulo was out the door. His face was red as he tugged at his collar and kicked off his shoes. They banged against the wall.

"Looking for the dog." Helena watched Paulo run by the window absently as she turned the stove off.

"Well, did you see it again?"

"No."

"So who cares about a stray dog! You forgot about your son!"

"*Sinto muito,* Nuno! Sorry! Paulo fine, though."

Nuno opened a beer and collapsed at the table. "Ms. Sanderson was nice about it at least," he said, staring blankly out the window.

Outside the sun was setting, and Helena thought she saw something black scamper into the woods across the street, but she couldn't be sure. "How old is she? She look really young."

Nuno just whistled to himself and tuned her out. Helena hated it when he did that.

After dinner she washed the dishes and Paulo played on the kitchen floor. Nuno was in the other room, watching television. Helena had to make lunches for tomorrow and try to keep her eyes on the window, so she hoisted Paulo up on the table.

His eyes were wide. He never got to sit up there.

"Paulo, you want play a game?"

He clapped his hands together. She used to make up games for him all the time.

"Look outside, okay? Tell me if you see a black dog."

He stared at her gravely, then turned to the window.

"If you see it, you yell, okay?"

Paulo pressed his forehead against the glass, watching intently.

Helena knew that soon it would be too dark. The dog, if he was smart enough, could blend with the shadows. And what would she do when she was in bed? How would she watch for him?

Nuno came into the kitchen and stared at Paulo, who was leaning against the window with both hands, his breath making a blurry circle.

"The hell is this?"

"Shhh," Helena said, "he's helping me look."

"For the dog?"

"Yes."

Nuno gave her a strange look. Then he chuckled and finished his wine, placing the dirty glass in the empty sink.

"Let's go to bed early," he said, winking at her. "I'm tired."

"After you see Ms. Sanderson, *certo?*" Helena murmured.

Nuno looked startled. "What?"

"Nothin'."

Paulo let out a squeal. "There!" he yelled, pointing.

"Good boy!" said Helena. But when she looked over his shoulder, staring out into the falling darkness, she couldn't see anything.

Before bed Helena went out with a candle to look at the footprints again. Nuno was brushing his teeth, and she'd already put Paulo to bed. He'd asked her if they could play the game again tomorrow.

"Depende," she'd said, pulling the covers up to his chin.

Outside she knelt down and smelled the deep mustiness of the soil. Above her their bedroom light shone, and she could see Nuno's profile framed in the window. She knew she should hurry. He liked Helena to be next to him when he climbed into bed. It was a cool night and she shivered in her nightgown, but just as she was about to go inside, she saw more marks in the dirt.

They were all over the place. New, freshly made prints, big and deep. Paulo had been right!

She followed the footprints through the rows of the garden excitedly until they disappeared across the lawn. As she stood barefoot in the wet grass, Helena was certain that tomorrow would be the day.

Upstairs, Nuno was in bed with the lights off. She wiped her feet on the rug and climbed in.

"What were you doing out there?" He gripped one of her thighs searchingly.

"The dog in the garden," she said, "it left footprints."

Nuno sighed. For a moment she thought maybe he was too tired tonight. "Tomorrow I'll be up early," she said. "Going to catch him."

"Great," he said sarcastically.

"Great," she said softly, and pictured the black dog in a big net, squirming and twitching. But where would she get the net? She thought of the yellow piece of paper, the list. It was folded in her apron. Nuno's hand hadn't left her thigh, and now it moved inward, pulling up her nightgown.

It was unavoidable. Almost every night. But this was her life, their life. And sometimes she even thought she could get there again, to the place where Mateo had taken her to so easily, the place where Nuno couldn't bring her anymore. But it was harder, now. It wasn't as though there hadn't been other men; when she was growing up, Helena had experimented with several men and even one woman, but she barely remembered them now. She *had* loved Nuno in the beginning—he was so obsessed with her, it was flattering. He'd cared too much, really. Had she felt that strongly about him, though, ever? She wasn't sure. But it didn't matter now.

Nuno pushed against her leg, now locked between his. He felt rubbery against her. His groaning grew louder, and he yanked the elastic from her hair. When he got on top, and his breath mixed with her hair, she turned her head to the side, away from the smell of toothpaste and red wine. Helena put herself outside, in the cool dark sand under Mateo's wooden boat, and summoned some sounds of her own. Hearing her, Nuno pushed harder and faster, and Helena pretended it was Mateo as his hand covered her mouth and she bit down on his fingers.

"Shhhh," said Nuno, "you'll wake Paulo."

So she quieted down and lay there, moving up and down lightly, listening to the rise and fall of the ocean and the faint screams of the gulls outside.

THE DOG

· III ·

When it was over and Nuno was snoring, Helena crept to the windowpane and pulled the rocking chair over to it. She stayed up all night, squinting into the blackness, watching for the dog. When the sun started to rise, she rushed downstairs.

Helena unplugged the coffee maker and put it on the counter opposite the window. Then she moved the toaster right next to it.

"*Hoje é o dia,*" she kept repeating to herself. "Today is the day."

Nuno came down with a puzzled look on his face. "Why is everything moved around?"

Helena shrugged and pointed out the window.

Nuno sat at the table and she served him his coffee with no milk and lots of sugar, the way he liked it, and set the *Providence Journal* in front of him. "Eggs coming," she said, leaning over the table to stare out the window.

Nuno studied the front page of the paper. "Wait, are you still looking for that fucking dog?"

"He in your *jardim!*"

"Helena, I've never even seen him."

"He'll shit all over!"

"What?"

Helena gritted her teeth. "Nuno! Yesterday you say—"

"Oh!" Nuno yelled, standing and pointing at the window, "Oh! I see him! Helena! I see him! There he is!"

Helena ran out the front door and charged toward the garden, almost tripping in her nightgown and bathrobe. "Where?" she called out from the lawn, "I don't see! Nuno! Nuno?"

But no one answered. Helena stopped yelling and looked around. There was a light morning mist steaming off of the lawn, brushing the plants. It looked like smoke, the way it drifted into the street and crept into the other lawns. She wished that there was someone to wave to, or that someone had seen the way her husband had tricked her. But the neighborhood was blank and silent.

Wait, were people watching her? Suddenly she felt the heat of a hundred eyes on her back, and she turned and hurried inside, her head down.

Paulo was sitting on Nuno's lap. "We played a joke on Mommy!" Nuno laughed loudly and ruffled Paulo's hair. "Didn't we, my boy?"

Helena served the rest of breakfast in silence and then sat in front of the window with her coffee. When they went upstairs to get ready to leave, she cleaned up slowly, watching the garden. The sun was beating down on it, drying out the soil. The mist was gone. She wondered if the eyes she'd felt digging into her back were gone too.

Nuno and Paulo bustled through the kitchen, and when Paulo came over to say goodbye, he put his arm around her neck and pulled until it hurt.

"What is he wearing?" Helena asked Nuno. She sniffed Paulo's shirt. "Is that dirty?"

Nuno shrugged, slurping coffee at the counter with his back to her. "You weren't up there to help."

"I was busy!"

Nuno shook his head at her, his mouth open, his coffee clenched in his hand. Helena put Paulo up on a chair near the window. "Watch for Mommy, now," she said. Then she walked over and stood right in front of Nuno.

"Why don't you understand?" she asked softly, staring at the tiny prickly hairs on his face, the yellowed tips of his teeth. "I'm *trying* to help you. *Este cão*—"

"Forget about the fucking dog! And how many times do I have to say? Speak English! You know where we are now, right?"

Nuno reached out and grabbed her waist, pressing his hands tightly into her hips. "I mean, what is it with you? What's wrong?" He leaned in. "Don't mention the dog again, okay? If I ever see it—which I won't—I'm going to kill it, because I don't ever want to hear about it again."

Helena craned her neck to look for Paulo. "But—"

"No buts. And pick up Paulo today, okay? I can't."

"Why not?"

"Because I have to stay late at work."

Helena nodded and looked back at Paulo. "Paulo, honey, you not watching," she whispered. Paulo was tracing his hand against the window, staring blankly at the ceiling. She thought he looked a little pale.

"What'd you say?"

Helena put her hand on Paulo's forehead to check it. But he couldn't stay home with her. Not on such an important day. Nuno would see. He would understand.

Nuno walked over and scooped Paulo up roughly into his arms, and for a second, the hand she had put on his forehead hung in the air limply. "Don't forget to pick him up," Nuno said. "We don't want him to be made fun of, Helena. People are going to *say* things about you. And I don't want them to."

He abruptly took her hand and squeezed it, then dropped it.

Helena looked at her hand, wondering why he had taken it like that. It was unlike him. He hadn't done anything romantic in years, and she neither regretted it nor expected it. But that touch almost brought everything back. For a second, sitting there, watching the wind blow through the tree that stood behind the garden, she felt like crying for the way they used to be, so long ago, in Lagos, or at least the way they'd thought that they were. Maybe their biggest problem had been the lack of honesty. And it had all started with her, and Mateo. She hated thinking about it, but like the eyes on her back, like the bees humming near her ears, she couldn't escape it.

Helena stared out the window at the garden so fiercely that her entire body twitched when Mr. and Mrs. Costa walked by with Riley. They passed by briskly, with Mr. Costa holding Riley's leash tightly as the dog ran back and forth across the street. He seemed particularly interested in their yard, and Helena even heard Mrs. Clark saying, "No, Riley, no."

Helena knew that Riley could smell the black dog. As she watched them disappear down the street, now arm in arm, Helena remembered her idea. She knew what she could do for Nuno to make things better. And maybe, just maybe, it would make her feel better too.

She found the yellow piece of paper crumpled up in her apron and sat down at the table, pushing plates and napkins aside. She began on the other side of the paper, with the date.

MAY 4TH.

Then she wrote, carefully, in English:

TODAY—I WILL CATCH THE BLACK DOG.

But how? She squeezed her eyes shut tightly, but they popped open. Her mind was blank. There were crumbs all over the table, crusts of toast, uneaten eggs. The sight of it made her feel slightly sick. She never let it get this bad. Sighing, she decided to clean the kitchen, do the laundry. Maybe something would come to her while she worked. Helena stood up and began dropping the food on one plate to throw away.

But then she realized how she could catch the dog.

It was like a bolt of lightning, or a flash of sunlight. She had it! Yes, this dog was smart. He'd shown her that, hadn't he? He'd been hiding in the shadows, he'd tricked Nuno and Paulo, he'd even made her look crazy. But he'd slipped up when he let Helena find his tracks. And now she had all day to outsmart him. And outsmart him she would.

Helena piled the scraps from breakfast in the middle of the table, then took everything out of the refrigerator so that she could choose exactly what the black dog would like to eat. She sliced two different blocks of cheese into a bowl. She found uncooked chicken, so she threw that in and added some leftover rabbit, and rice. They had more for tonight in the freezer—after she finished with this, she'd cook, do the chores, everything. She'd feel so good when this was over with! Then she remembered that dogs love milk, so she dumped a carton of milk on top.

The whole time, Helena kept stealing looks at the garden. But she wasn't that worried anymore, because she could get the dog to come out anytime. She had a plan, she had bait, now she just needed to get it done before Nuno came home. While she let the food sit in the bowl—she thought it smelled good, it was making her hungry—she checked the time. It was one, so she had three hours before she needed to pick up Paulo. On the yellow paper, she wrote:

HOW TO CATCH IT (1 O'CLOCK)

Helena sat down and stared at the paper for a while, chewing her pencil. She remembered that a few years back they'd had a mouse problem, and Nuno had laid traps filled with peanut butter to catch them. Once, after he'd gone to work, she'd heard the snap of a trap and raced down to the kitchen to find one of the mice squirming and squeaking across the linoleum, his back crushed by the metal bar. She'd waited all day for Nuno to get rid of it, but she couldn't stop watching it struggle. It would lie there motionless for hours as she sat and sipped her coffee, and just when she thought it had given up, it would twitch its entire body violently. Pleading with her. Staring up with its beady eyes until she had to leave the room. But she always came back.

"Why didn't you just kill it? Were you that scared?" Nuno had asked. He forced a laugh, but then stared at her, frowning. Then he put on a pair of gloves, put the mouse in a paper bag, brought it out to the garage, and stepped on it.

Helena took the peanut butter out. But when the dog came, how would she actually catch it? A big net would work. But she might struggle with the net, and the dog could chew through it. What if he got angry? What if he went for her leg, growling and snapping, his teeth sharp? She wished she had a dog-sized mouse trap, but she didn't. She decided to go ahead with the first part of her plan, and see what happened. It felt like the right thing to do.

With a wooden spoon Helena scooped pieces of meat and cheese onto the earth and then poured the rest out. The milk sank into the soil, and the food fell with a damp thud. She spooned globs of peanut butter and smeared it on all of the plants. She knew the spring rains would come and take it all away soon, but when she was done she really liked the way the yellow and brown food mixture was spread neatly on the soil, with the peanut butter weighing heavily on the small plants' leaves.

Helena went down to the basement to look around. She brought outside a heavy shovel that Nuno used for work around the yard, a coil of thick rope covered in dust and spider webs, some nails, a hammer, and a two-by-four.

She laid everything quietly on the grass in the front yard. She didn't know what to do when the dog finally came. And honestly, now he could run out any minute. Any minute! Helena's heart started pounding like it did at night in bed with Nuno. *Deus!* It frustrated her that she'd come this far but she had no idea how to finish the job. Her back and forehead grew hot and cold. The food was baking in the sun, and she could smell the ocean breeze lifting the smell of hot dogs and sour milk from the garden and taking it somewhere else.

Then, across the street, she saw something moving.

It was the old Italian couple who lived two streets over, the Baccaris. As they walked by, Mr. Baccari ventured a wave.

"Afternoon," he called out, and he and his wife slowed to look at the garden.

"A beautiful day, right?" Helena asked.

They moved slowly by, not answering. Mrs. Baccari held her fingers over her nose, and Mr. Baccari cocked his head at Helena before they disappeared down the street.

Helena's head began to ache, right at the temples. She rubbed at them with her fingers. Things had been going so well, she thought, as she looked around. But her feet were speckled with mud. She was still in her nightgown. If she went inside to change, though, she knew that the dog would come, eat all the food, and never come back. What time had it been when she first saw the black dog? She couldn't remember! Everything felt hazy, and the eyes were back, prodding at her shoulders. Probably staring through windows at her right now, wondering just what the hell she was doing.

She thought about how Nuno had said he would kill him. She thought about Mateo, and what Nuno had done. What she had never been able to ask him about. She thought of the way Mateo used to touch her so lightly, almost as if with a woman's hands. Almost like the wind right now, drifting up her nightgown, cool on her thighs. The drumming in her temples grew faster. Nuno was going to kill the dog anyway. If she caught it, she would have to keep it somewhere until he got home. In the house, where it would do as it pleased? Roped up somewhere? She imagined trying to tie it up, with the Costas and the Baccaris staring over her shoulder, laughing.

But if Nuno came home and Helena had taken care of the dog, he would approve. One less thing for him to have to do. He would take her in his arms and apologize. He would know that he'd been wrong about her all along.

Helena picked up the shovel and practiced swinging it a few times. This would be quicker, and if someone happened to see her, then that was that. They'd be impressed, even, that she was dealing with this herself. She couldn't picture Mrs. Baccari, with her skinny arms and cautious way of walking, even *holding* a shovel.

A few seagulls had gathered in the grass to feast, and they anxiously flapped their wings as she ran toward them, yelling. She watched one of them settle in a tree, a pink piece of hot dog hanging from his yellow beak. Then she peered around. Where could she hide? Toward the rear of the garden there were a few crooked bushes that grew between their house and the small shack behind it. Helena crept over and carefully lay on her stomach, under cover. The shovel was at her side, and she'd strung the rope around her shoulders.

All there was left to do was wait. She figured it was around two-thirty. Nuno wouldn't be home 'til later. Her stomach, pressed into the grass and dirt, tensed with excitement. She could feel the wind lifting the back of her nightgown up, but she didn't care. No one would see her, so low to the ground, so hidden. She needed to stay perfectly still and wait.

— ◠ —

Helena's back was stiffening, and she was beginning to think her plan wasn't going to work. Clovers and tufts of grass tickled her nose, and her leg was falling asleep. Her mind was wandering, so it didn't feel real when she saw something trotting into her line of vision, its head bobbing back and forth. *The black dog!* Helena pulled the air through her lungs as slowly as she could. Her chest itched, the prickly lawn pressed through her nightgown. But there he was, scampering along, his nose to the ground, the white flicker of his tail lifted to the sky. He was bigger than she'd thought! She watched him run through the street, his paws skittering in the dry sand, then slip across their yard, stopping to sniff and lick the bowl she had left out. He paused at the top of the cellar stairs, where the bulkhead was open. Would he go in? She held onto the shovel tightly. She hadn't considered that he might! But he turned then, his tongue hanging out, and made right for the garden. He started at the first row, sniffing and then licking and chewing. He tried the peanut butter, and then his tongue flared pink as he tried over and over to lick his nose clean. Helena tried to stop but it was no use, she couldn't help it. She began to laugh. This was what she'd been waiting for. She rose through the bushes until she was up on her knees.

The dog stopped. He lifted his slender face and looked at her, his mouth dripping. They locked eyes, and it was almost as if he was smiling at her. Then he sniffed the air and went back to rooting through the soil, his tail wagging.

Helena stood up and walked lightly, silently. When she was behind him, the soil wet under her feet, the warm, rotten smell all around her, she raised the shovel over her head with both hands, watching as the dog dug frantically for more food, panting. At the second that she brought the shovel down with all of her strength, the black dog sensed it, and he looked up at her.

He lay on his side, his tongue hanging from the side of his mouth. One leg was still lazily pedaling, and his ear was cut and pink with blood. He tried a few times to right himself, to stand, but he fell back down, on his right side, growing weaker. He whimpered the whole time, a high-pitched, anxious tune, and that was why she hit him again.

There was blood on the shovel. It wasn't really red, more of a dark purple. Helena wiped it well on the grass and put it back in the cellar. When she went back over to the dog, he was lying in a heap on the ground, his fur wet. Nuno would be so proud of her. Paulo, when he was older and realized what she'd done, would be proud of her. As she stood over him, a station wagon passed by, slowing down. There were children in the backseat, and they pressed their faces against the window. Helena waved, grinning as the car sped up.

She decided to drag the dog away from the garden and over toward the driveway. She'd leave him on the edge of the lawn and hopefully Nuno would take care of it. After all, she'd done everything else, right?

THE DOG

Helena had already started dinner when she heard the car in the driveway. She waited to hear the doors swing open as she cut potatoes into slices. She knew it would be hard for Nuno to see the black dog in the darkness. But she felt a little tremor of excitement well up inside.

Nuno closed the door behind him and immediately walked to the fridge. He popped a beer and sniffed the air. "Smells good in here," he said. "Where's Paulo?"

Helena's stomach dropped. Nothing ever went completely right.

"Paulo! Paulo!" Nuno called, walking into the hallway, banging on the wall. He turned back to her, puzzled. "Where'd he go? Outside?"

Helena put down the knife. It would be better to just get it out there. "Nuno, I—I forgot. Did his teacher call you? I didn't—"

Nuno's eyes darkened, his mouth opened. He punched the wall and dropped his beer. They both watched it pump foam onto the floor.

"How—*how* do you forget about your son, *again*? *How* do you just forget?" He stepped toward her. "I bet they were calling here all day. Why didn't you pick up? What if something happened to him, Helena? What if something *happened*?"

He picked his beer up and finished it viciously, then chucked it toward the sink. It bounced back to the floor. Nuno put one hand on the counter and breathed deep, his head down. Then he looked straight at her and spoke quietly. "You know what? Then it's all your fault! All your fucking fault."

"I'll go get him," she said quickly. She wanted to tell him about the dog *so badly.*

Nuno closed his eyes. "What's wrong with you? It's like you've lost it or something. You're not even a good mother anymore."

Helena winced, her finger finding her temple. "I'll go get him, Nuno. I said I'll get him."

"Nope, you'll just screw it up. I'll go. I worked all day just so I can drive around all night. *Jesus Cristo.* Ugh, and what is that red shit all over you?" He glared at her and then his eyes faltered for a second. "What—"

Nuno reached out to touch her and then hesitated.

"Look," she said, and pointed out the window. "Follow me, okay?"

Helena jogged out the door. "Come on," she called, "Come, Nuno, come see!"

Nuno grabbed his keys and slammed the door on his way out. Helena was standing at the corner of the lawn where she'd left him, and Nuno walked over, muttering. Helena put her hand on his back and rubbed it as they both stared down at the dog in the dim light.

"I'm sorry about Paulo," Helena started, "but—"

She pointed down proudly. The dog's neck was pointed awkwardly down and one of his front paws was twisted beneath him. Helena had tried to arrange him as best as she could.

Nuno couldn't look at the dog. He jerked his eyes away and stared at his wife's nightgown, at the brownish stains that crept down to her ankles. He looked out over at the garden, where in the gray light of dusk flies buzzed and seagulls squawked.

Helena's eyes were hopeful, bright. "The black dog, Nuno. I got him."

Nuno wrinkled his nose as if he'd smelled something bad, then stepped away and surveyed the darkening street, the houses that were now lit up like lanterns. "How—" he tried, but the word sounded feeble.

Helena put her hand around his waist. "Don't worry. It was easy," she said. "It was nothing, really."

Nuno pulled away. He knelt before the dog and paused there, hands on his knees. Then he gave his head a little shake and stood up. "It's not even black," he whispered. "Helena, did you—"

"Now do you believe me?" she said, smiling. Her teeth glinted in the dying light.

Nuno avoided her and walked toward the car, stumbling a little bit in the shadows.

"Okay," he said, holding up his hand. "Okay." He breathed deeply, as if he thought he might be sick, but then he shook his head.

"I've got to go get Paulo," he called out, his voice shaking just a little. "Helena? Listen to me." He cleared his throat. The seagulls were fighting over the scraps behind them, flapping their wings in the cool air.

Helena stood there next to the dog, waiting for him to finish. She reached down and moved one of the paws over. That was better.

THE DOG

When Nuno spoke again, his voice was stronger. "Helena, put the dog behind the house right now. Do it quickly. I'll get rid of it later. Wash up, finish making dinner, and then go to bed. I don't want to see you when I get back. I don't want to see you, hear me? I'll tell the boy you're sick."

Nuno slammed the door and started the car. In the flash of headlights the dog shone in the slick grass. Then the tires screeched and his car disappeared into the darkness.

Helena stood there, wiping her hands on her nightgown, listening to the sound of the engine fade out into the night. Then she sat down in the shadows of the driveway. At least for now, everything was silent. No one was watching her. She would stay there for a few minutes, waiting. Thinking about what to do next. Then, she would do what Nuno said.

jerusalem

Hailey sips her coffee and squints at the horizon through the window. We pass boarded-up clam shacks and beach cabins as we speed down Old Succotash Road. Even the salt pond, skirted by patches of cracking ice, looks gray and deserted.

"Scott?"

I pretend to be lost in the lifeless November sky, the limp power lines, the boats that are stranded in brown backyards and covered up for the coming winter.

She sighs happily and taps her hands on the wheel. "Well, Dr. Rich *did* say that this trip might inspire some deep thought."

I close my eyes tightly and watch the colors. Someone told me in college that the red splotches that you see are actually your own blood, flowing beneath your eyelids. It was one of those stoned conversations that I don't remember much of. Is that true? It doesn't matter. None of it does. I can feel Hailey's eyes on me. She's smiling. *Deep thought?* All I can think about lately is getting out of here.

A few days ago, half drunk, rummaging through the closet for more of Emily's stuff to give away—what her idiot shrink calls the "cleansing process"—I found my dad's pictures of Brazil. Green water, thatched roofs on the beach, stretches of golden sand dotted with brown bodies. He'd never really said anything about it when I was younger, just that he'd traveled around "like a damn bum" and was glad that he was done with it. But I don't believe that for a second. I know he went to South America, to Europe. I bet he had the time of his life over there. For a while there,

I think my dad and I both thought that I'd go abroad too, to play soccer. But that's over with now, too. Way over.

But Brazil? No one would know me there. There'd be none of those really deliberate handshakes at the supermarket, from people I never knew that well. There'd be no whispers echoing behind my back when I walk into the Mews Tavern, or the Mist, for a beer. I'm not saying I'd want to forget anything—I never could. But I do know that Hailey and I can't fight the fact anymore that whatever we had is gone. All that is left is the same heavy silence that is filling the car right now. And I need to get *out*.

In the empty parking lot, dirt and sand crunches under the tires. A few pebbles kick up and rattle against the bottom of the car.

"Jesus, slow down!"

Hailey looks hurt, and I feel a pang of regret. But we're gonna talk—and probably fight—eventually, right? Isn't that what this is all about, this whole idea of her bringing me here? Some kind of confrontation—with the past, or with each other? My dad told me when I was nine or ten that when I got in a fight, I should square off and throw the first punch, a jab, while protecting my face with my right. Throwing the first punch, he said, was key.

Hailey carefully puts the car in park and her hand finds my arm, her fingers warm. She's trying harder today. That's pretty obvious.

"Sorry. I was just scared." I try to laugh. It feels forced.

The lines on her forehead crease; she purses her lips and nods to herself. I know she believes in this shit. I know she has faith in the mighty mind of Dr. Elizabeth Rich. I can't even believe that's her real name. She's absolutely *getting* rich off the cash we're paying her to sit and talk to my wife every week. This week, I guess the objective was to get me to come with her to the beach, to *this* beach. And I had to hand it to her, Hailey had been persistent. I guess she always was. Our arguments before this happened—God, what did we argue about in those days? Sex? Money?—usually ended with me giving in to her. But I find myself not letting her have the last word anymore. I come at her hard. Sometimes I'm such an asshole that I scare myself.

We slam the doors and the ocean breeze is cold on my face. I've forgotten how much I used to love that smell. Hailey ties her hair back, then pushes a red baseball hat down on her head. "I want you to try today," she says. "Can you do that? Can you try?"

She looks at me patiently. I lean down to tie my shoe. It feels like we're both on a tightrope now, walking single file, arms outstretched. I don't know who's in front. Probably her.

"Scott?"

I nod. Hailey beams and walks away from me. She's humming a song I know but can't place.

We can't see the water yet, but we can hear it. Crashing, sucking at the shore hungrily. I jog to catch up with her. "What is that?"

"What?"

"That song—what song is that?" I almost have to keep jogging to stay in stride with her. She hasn't given up on the gym like me; instead, her workouts have intensified. She pedals like crazy in those spin classes. At night, a lot of times she does crunches on her exercise ball in front of the TV. I sit behind her, drinking cans of Coors Lite and ignoring her.

She looks puzzled. "I don't know. It was on the radio or something."

"That's weird. You're singing it, and you don't even know what song it is? I just thought . . . I mean, I know it. I know I recognize it, and—"

"Well, we didn't come here to talk about this song, though, right?"

"What? No, I just thought . . ."

"I don't know what song it is, Scott."

"Oh. Okay." I kick a beer can, and it sails through the air in a cloud of pebbles and sand. "Goal!" I yell, raising my arms over my head.

Hailey shakes sand from her hair. Her face registers a trace of annoyance, but she pushes it away. That didn't take long, did it?

"Let's walk," she says, composed again. She links arms with me.

I still don't know how she doesn't understand. I don't want to try again. I don't want another kid. I'm so sick of all the books on grief and mourning that she reads, sick of the way she folds the corners of the pages and leaves them on the kitchen counter for me. I don't want psychotherapy or theories or analysis. I'd rather be told simple things—starting with *why*. Because every night and every morning I relive that day, running through every movement, every word, each detail in my head. If I'm drunk enough, I can almost enjoy the good parts. I can almost forget the ending, where it all went to hell.

As we walk down the path of wooden slats, Hailey lets go of my arm and offers me her hand. I stare at her purple mitten and then take it in mine. Behind us, seagulls flap their wings in the quickening wind, urging me on. She squeezes twice, leading me out onto the beach.

I look to the left immediately. A reflex, I guess. I haven't been back here since it happened. But suddenly, here I am. Shit. *Here I am.* "Should have brought a bottle of wine or something, huh?"

Hailey looks back at me, shakes her head.

"It's just pretty here, you know? Be nice to sit." I trail off.

She doesn't say anything. The lifeguard chairs are all stored away, and near the water, the sand is hard and wet and nearly black. We walk toward the tiny beach town of Jerusalem silently, our hands tightly clasped, the waves blue and gray and swollen. The wind is picking up and the sky grows darker. I try once or twice to point at the darkening horizon, but Hailey doesn't notice my warnings, and my finger waves uselessly in the wind. I know a squall can come quick, though.

The nameless tune hums in my head, the drums kick softly. Fragments of dreams begin to whisper in my ears. I guess, really, I *have* been back here. I come back whenever I'm able to get to sleep, which isn't that often. But in my dreams, Emily scampers through the beach grass in front of me, just out of reach.

The ocean streams forward and lashes at my foot, soaking it.

"Shit! It's so cold!" We let go of each other, pushing forward into the wind, Hailey's jacket rippling, my arms crossed. I reach to touch her lower back, to help guide her, but then take my hand away. She bites her lip and I know she's trying to decide what she wants to say. She probably didn't count on the strong wind in our faces, the grinding of the waves. She probably envisioned us sitting next to each other under the setting sun. But we're here, and this is the time and place to do it. If she still wants to.

As we reach the private beach, way at the end, the wind rips Hailey's hat off of her head. She cries out and gives chase, but it skips and spins away from her. I should run and help her. Instead, I look down at my empty hand and flex it. Hailey always joked that my hands were too soft, that she preferred men with rougher palms that were torn up from hard labor. I laughed, but wondered if there was some truth to it.

Hailey's long, skinny legs bend awkwardly under her as she lunges. "She slides on her knees in the wet sand, then holds her hat up triumphantly.

I walk over and stand over her without any idea of what to do. Her hair escapes from her hat and hangs down her back.

"Got it!" she says. When she looks up at me, her face is innocent. I'd like to kneel next to her. But I can't even get myself to smile. Instead, my skin stings. I'm starting to really hate this wind, how it won't let up for a second. My right foot aches, wet and cold.

Past Hailey, the waves are churning white and slamming against the rocks. I want to throw rocks into the water and the wind. I want to run to the warm silence of the car, drive away from this, and crack a beer at home. Alone.

"Scott? Pull me up?"

Hailey reaches out, but I just stand there, rooted to the sand. Why did she bring me here? Was it to remind me how much of this was my fault?

"Scott?"

Hailey stands up finally, pushing herself off the ground. Her smile fades, her eyes fall down.

"You said you would try. You said you would. I don't know what else—"

She turns toward a jetty and walks quickly away from me, burying her head in the rush of wind.

"Hailey." I don't yell her name. I doubt she even hears me.

I follow her for a while, not speeding up, not slowing down. I watch her body—the way her legs slide back and forth, her thin thighs just barely touching. How her back stays so straight. I'm fascinated by the way she moves with such willingness and desire.

The shore is running out. To our left are houses with perfect ocean views, their shingles weathered and torn by salt air. Ahead of us the long jetty stretches out to sea, usually speckled with men carrying fishing lines and buckets. Across the water I can barely make out the fishing port of

Galilee, where restaurants are closed and masts shiver in the wind. Everything is empty and dark. Used up.

As I get closer to the jetty, the rain hits my forehead, the back of my neck. I've been so focused on watching Hailey that I haven't noticed the clouds that have pushed in. Hailey hesitates at the slippery rocks, the spray of the ocean and the rain making everything blur together. Then she carefully climbs up.

Perched there on the jetty, crouching on one of the broad, flat rocks, I can tell that she's deciding which way to go. On a calm day, if you pay attention to where you step, the walk isn't bad. But today the water is snapping at both sides, and I'm sure the surfaces are slick. There are dark spaces between the rocks where, if you crouch down, you can sometimes see giant crabs lurking. I showed Emily once, a few summers ago, and she yelped and jerked back against my chest when she saw the pink and white twitch of legs.

Hailey hasn't looked back at me. I bet she's thinking that whatever this plan was, it hasn't worked. Did she really think it would? I wipe the rain off of my face, but it just keeps coming, cold and driving. Hailey said the other night that my face looked different now, more serious or something. I forget the word she used. I didn't tell her that I think she looks and *acts* different now. That I feel like she's not the woman I married.

She takes her hat off and stuffs it in her pocket, then steps nimbly across the rocks, her arms up for balance. I tense. She goes from rock to rock, her confidence growing, her feet light. The further she goes, the deeper the water is, the bigger the waves are that crash on either side. Don't fall, I think, just don't fall.

I barely see her stumble, arms flailing, but my heart skips and I stop walking toward her, as if my movement could jinx her. She catches herself just before she tumbles, then she stands there, hands on her hips, getting her balance back. Slowly, she kneels down, the water on each side of her splashing with the wind and the rain and the growing swells.

I stay there, my hands in my pockets, my feet still stuck in the sand. Thunder growls in the distance. Fog begins to sift down.

I know that if I were to touch Hailey's back right now, her muscles would be taut and rigid. If we weren't here, but naked together in bed, and in love, I'd kiss her bare shoulder, breathing in the acidic scent of the glossy soaps that she's always used, the ones that come in small fishnet bundles from the health-foods store in Wakefield.

She looks so small up there. *I still love you,* I think. *I do. Please don't fall. Just don't fall.* I wish I was in front of her, leading her. I'd dig in and scramble up the rocks the way I did with my father when I was young, and Hailey could follow me the way that I used to follow him. If I fell back he would be right behind me to push me forward, as if it had never happened.

Hailey is on one knee, paralyzed. She still hasn't looked at me, and I wonder for a second if she even knows if I'm here. The waves pound at the rocks all around her. If she stumbles and hits her head, slides into the water that's brown and heavy with seaweed and yellow foam, she could drown.

She could drown.

My feet slap the sand as I sprint and hoist myself up, my hands sliding off the rock. The stone slides beneath my feet but I move quickly, recklessly, stubbing my toe, banging my ankle, once falling to my knees and cutting my hands on barnacles.

Hailey grows larger in my blurry eyes, and then I'm balancing on the small section of rock next to her. She still doesn't turn. I put my hands on her shoulders, and she looks up blankly, as if she doesn't recognize me. As if I could be anyone. We stand there, soaked and trembling in the wind, and the Block Island Ferry emerges from the fog. But it's not summer, and there's no one waving from the deck into the sunshine. The giant boat clangs its way by, and then there is nothing left but the swirling wake.

There's no traction here, my feet want to slip out from under me. I dig my hands into her shoulders so she knows that if she moves, I might fall. She does nothing, just hunches away from me, her head down. She might be crying, I can't tell. I press harder and she pushes me back so fiercely that I nearly lose balance. But I don't. Instead I somehow haul her up and hold her close to me. She looks shocked, and we have to lean into each other, face to face, so we don't get sucked out to sea.

JERUSALEM

· 129 ·

"You took her away," Hailey screams finally. Her voice is faint, carrying with the wind. "You took her away, Scott! *My daughter!*"

She pulls away and I let her go. Then I turn and begin to walk away.

"It's not my fault," I think I hear her yell as I jog down the beach. My feet are soaked through and numb. Hailey is still on the jetty, all wrapped up, small and thin. The storm is right on top of us now, and I wonder why they hadn't said anything about it on the local weather this morning. Maybe they did, and I just missed it. I have trouble remembering normal things these days. I remember things like the fluorescent lights of the children's hospital and the way Hailey looked at me when she drove us away from the beach that morning after we lost Emily. The way she sobbed and gripped the steering wheel with one hand, how the other hand dug into my wrist so hard it left a bruise.

"I didn't even get to say goodbye," was all that she said that day, her teeth clenched. The veins in her forehead pressed angrily against the skin.

What a joke. I know she resented Emily for getting sick. I saw the look on Hailey's face at the beach that day, the shine of her teeth. She has to know that I saw her face. And afterward, the way she kept saying that she thought things would start to get easier? These are the things I don't forget. These are the moments I bring with me everywhere.

And what the hell had she been talking about this morning? That she thought a trip to Europe or California, even, would be good for us? An escape, she called it?

I look back down the shore. I've come about three hundred yards. Hailey is in the same place. She hasn't moved. I want to go home. I'll leave without her. The keys are in the car.

Almost as if she can read my mind, Hailey stands and turns around, heading back down the rocks. I watch her navigate the cracks and the holes. She doesn't slip once. Then she jumps to the beach, touches one hand to the sand, and looks around for me.

She might be calling my name, but her words are swept away with the rain. Hailey begins to try to run toward me, digging in and fighting the currents of wind, but she barely moves. It is as if she is drowning. Or learning to swim.

a simple thing

PAULO · 1976

· SATURDAY ·

Paulo was almost sixteen, but he'd understood since he was eleven. It was after his first dream—which he wished had been about Isabella but was about Jenny, a girl from CCD class—that he realized what the sounds *really* were. In his dream he found himself on top of Jenny on the floor of a bright, crowded school hallway, his hands squeezing the round breasts she kept tucked behind fuzzy gray sweaters. That white-hot feeling came from nowhere, spiking in his thighs and spine, and he tensed on the slippery edge of waking. Jenny opened her mouth, her breath hot on his neck.

"No," she said faintly, "no!" Paulo's eyes blinked open in the dark. The voice grew louder. "Stop, Nuno! Stop!"

He rolled off his sagging mattress with a thud, clutching his dick, and the house went abruptly silent in response. Hours later Paulo woke up on the floor with his brittle underwear glued to his thighs, proof that he hadn't imagined it.

Tonight, when the noises started, Paulo was already thinking about Isabella. A few hours before, they'd been were pressed together in the back of a movie theater, her legs wrapped so tightly around one of his that it fell asleep. But he didn't even think of moving away.

Paulo immediately sat up and clicked on the clock radio, static twitching as he played with the dial. It had to be music, not talk, and it had to have a full sound in order to work. Rock and Roll worked better than jazz or classical. A singer who screamed, like Robert Plant, worked pretty good to cover up most of it. Unless it was one of those Led Zeppelin songs that suddenly cut away to a quiet part, like "Babe I'm Gonna Leave You." Paulo loved Zeppelin, though he only owned one album, his tattered copy of *Led Zeppelin IV*.

"It's Only Rock 'n Roll (But I Like It)" by the Stones was on, and he put the volume about halfway up, clasped his hands under his head, and instead of concentrating on Isabella, tried to go over each mistake he had made at soccer practice. For each missed trap and bad pass, he imagined what he could've done differently.

Paulo started to drift off, his thoughts blinking on and off with the rattling drum beat of The Who's "Squeezebox," but tonight he thought he could still hear the squeak of the mattress, the breathing and whispering. But maybe it was all in his head? Paulo wished he had the balls to bring it up with his dad. His mom acted different in the mornings afterward, too. She was too nice to him, and she mostly just stared out the window into the yard, where seagulls paced and shat in the early light. He felt bad for her, but he didn't think there was anything he could do. Before going to school he'd hug her goodbye, even at his age, and her body crumpled into his. Paulo always had to let go first.

It was funny. Late at night, when he felt trapped between the noises and the hiss of the radio, Paulo imagined waking up in Lagos. He'd never been there, but he just made it up, based on pictures he'd seen. He'd learn to surf, and spend hours lying in a hammock as dark-skinned women with long black hair sunbathed topless next to him. Sometimes, Paulo imagined taking Isabella to Lagos for their honeymoon. They'd drink Sagres from tall icy glasses—the beer that there were always commercials for on Rádio e Televisão de Portugal—and it would be so much better than the sour cans of Busch-Lite and Natural-Light that burned his throat. They'd watch the colored fishing boats set sail off of the coast, the water the same green as a Rolling Rock bottle. Some nights Paulo woke up still clinging to visions of climbing the pink and rust-red rock cliffs that jutted out over the water. Sometimes his mom was walking beside him on the beach, smiling for once.

In those dreams, his dad was nowhere to be found.

"Do you think we're weird?" Isabella's voice sounded thin. Paulo was sprawled in bed, the phone pressed to his ear.

"No," he said, "you're weird." She laughed and changed the subject but Paulo was only half listening. He wanted to grab the box so he could look at the pictures, but his legs were beat from practice and he didn't feel like getting up.

"What if your mom or dad find them?" she whispered.

"They never would," Paulo said. He wrapped the phone cord around his thumb and it began to turn purple.

They had only taken pictures a few times. Paulo was drunk one night and he and Isabella were fooling around, and he asked her if she'd let him take some. She wasn't that into it at first, but now she liked it even more than he did. Paulo had gotten the idea when he was looking through his dad's magazines. He didn't think his dad knew that he'd found them, but maybe he did. What could he say anyway? Inside one of the magazines was a picture of this waitress Paulo had seen before at the club, Kim. She looked better in the picture than she did in real life, that was for sure. There was just something about a picture of a real girl, too, that made it better than those perfect models in *Playboy*.

They'd used a Polaroid camera, and Paulo had kept every photo, except for the one Isabella took for herself. So far he had seven, and he kept them hidden in between the dusty baseball cards that he didn't want anymore, stowed under his bed. Nuno had collected cards when they first moved here, and he said some of them would be worth something someday. Paulo wasn't sure.

Most of the pictures were blurry. Sometimes Isabella's skin looked orange, other times it glowed white in the light from the flash. In one she was fully clothed, in a few others she was posing in her underwear, and in another, on a night when they'd both gotten really drunk on vodka and fruit punch at Chloe's house, Isabella was almost totally naked.

Paulo wasn't really in any of them. There was one where he'd held the camera with his left hand and his right arm was outstretched into the frame, his hand over one of her breasts. It was his favorite. The only time he'd ever really used them was two weekends ago when Isabella went away for the weekend with her parents. Paulo had stood with them spread out on his bed, his pants around his ankles and his ears cocked to hear his parents' car pull into the driveway.

"Did you have fun last night?" Isabella asked. The phone was making Paulo's ear ache.

"Yeah, of course."

"So, I think I'm ready."

"Yeah?"

"I *think* so."

"When?" His mind raced. "My parents are going to my grandpa's on Saturday night."

Silence. Had he been too anxious?

"Maybe," she finally whispered.

They said goodnight. The house was perfectly silent. For the first time, Paulo wondered if his parents could be listening to him.

· MONDAY ·

"It's in your blood," Nuno said. "You'll get it." He pulled the car around and squinted in the late August sun, then checked the time, tapping his fingers on the dashboard clock. He worked in an auto parts factory, but he was going in late today so he could bring Paulo to the field.

"You're ready this year," he said, but Paulo wasn't convinced. It was the exact same thing that he told him last year. He hadn't even been able to eat his eggs in the morning.

Paulo watched some of the guys pass the ball back and forth on the sprawling field. Next to their car, a bunch of older guys pulled up in a Jeep, blaring the Doors. Paulo stared straight ahead.

I'm not going to "get it," he wanted to say. *I will never be as good as you want me to be, dad. Even if I make the team this year, I'll never be a star.* He'd watched other kids "get it," and he'd seen the way his father looked at them. They were heroes, and Paulo wasn't. They'd drive home to bright kitchens, shiny tile floors, and steaming plates of spaghetti or take-out pizza. Paulo wouldn't. He and his dad would go home to their small house near the ocean, where his mom would be camped out in the living room, smoking menthols and watching Portuguese soap operas. The three of them would eat chicken and rice in the dim light of the kitchen, and later that night Paulo would fall asleep with the music on so he could only vaguely hear the riptide of gasps and whispers.

"*Acalme-se, querida,*" his mom might say in Portuguese, her voice flat, "*acalme-se.*" He wondered if anyone else at practice had to listen to their parents doing it at night.

"Paulo, you ready? What are you doing? Get out. They're waiting for you!" His dad's English was sliced into short pieces. It made him sound angry. But Paulo had been to the club with him, and listened to the way Portuguese rolled from his mouth. It was softer somehow, effortless. And it was usually followed by a wink, or a laugh from the guys. But the man that Paulo had seen his father become at the club seemed to disappear when they left the dark bar.

"Nice field," Nuno remarked. The lines beneath his eyes, under his glasses, deepened as he stared out the window. "We used to play in the street without shoes. So now? You have no excuse."

Paulo could always feel it coming on, setting in his jaw, stiffening in his bones. It was like stepping into another skin, like when he was younger and he'd lose a board game and then suddenly flip the board over, the pieces smashing and scattering.

"Get out. I'm gonna go park so I can come back and watch."

Paulo pretended to tie his shoes. "I'm going," he said through clenched teeth. "You're not staying!"

"Watch your mouth." Nuno shook his finger in Paulo's face but couldn't hide his grin. "That old Portuguese temper, just like your old man. Maybe it'll do you some good out there."

Paulo's mom noticed first. It had been over a month since he had met Isabella at the beach, but he'd managed to keep it a secret. His plan was to keep her away from his parents for as long as possible. But his mom caught him spinning around in front of the mirror in our hallway in the morning, tucking and then un-tucking his shirt.

"Look at this! Paulo must have a *noiva*!" She switched to rattling Portuguese, her hair in a towel, knocking on the bathroom door. "Nuno!"

Paulo rolled his eyes and stomped into his room. "Mom, stop!"

Nuno flung open the door, soaking wet in a green towel, thick black hair matted against his chest.

"What is it? What?" he cried, his eyes narrowed.

"Paulo has a girlfriend!" Helena announced.

"Is this true?" he asked. "What's her name?"

Paulo shook his head and turned away from the wet heat coming from the bathroom.

"The girl that called last night, Paulo, is that her? Isabel? Isabella?" Helena's face lit up.

Nuno grinned crookedly, slicked his wet hair back with both hands, and slammed the door shut again. Paulo heard him humming to himself in the shower.

"I want to meet her, Paulo!" yelled his mother as he headed for the kitchen. "When we meet her?"

· WEDNESDAY ·

He'd made the team.

He wasn't sure if it was all the running on the beach this summer or what, but he'd been playing better than last year, that was for sure. When he could stay angry—at his father, at Isabella, at anyone—he could do all right as a defender. Sliding for the ball in the dirt, jamming his shoulders into people if they ran by him. Coach said he had good hustle. And after tryouts, Jessie Stokes, probably the best player on the varsity team, asked if Paulo wanted to go to his party and hang out. Those guys had barely talked to Paulo before this!

Last fall, Paulo had been so scared to tell his dad that he didn't make it that he waited outside the house in the rain for an hour, until his mom came home. But today he barged right in. Nuno was sitting at the table drinking a beer.

"About time!" he exclaimed when Paulo told him. Paulo shrugged as if it were no big deal and sat down on the tile floor to peel off his damp socks and shin guards.

"Will you start?"

"No, not now." He stood and the dried dirt from the field crackled on his legs. He rubbed at it. "Maybe later, though."

Nuno finished the glass and rubs his stomach. "Helena," he cried, "the men are hungry out here!" He stood and looked incredulously at the empty stove and the package of frozen chicken sweating on the counter. "Where the hell is your mother? She's not even started yet?"

Paulo leaned over the counter to look at the sports page. The Red Sox had gotten beat by Detroit six to one.

"Bunch of bums," Nuno said, pointing to the paper. "Helena!" he yelled again, slamming his hand on the table.

Then he surprised Paulo by striding over, clapping his shoulder hard enough to sting, and pulling him to his chest. He smelled of beer and Old Spice aftershave. "You just need a chance," he muttered, patting the back of Paulo's neck roughly.

Helena walked into the kitchen in her bathrobe, carrying a bottle of Coke and a pack of Parliaments. Before she started cooking, she went to the windowsill where she kept her pills. She told Paulo that she took them for her stomach pains. But whenever the topic of her visits to the doctor came up, Paulo noticed that his dad wouldn't look him in the eye, and he kind of shook his head once, real fast, as if he was trying to erase something.

"Supper will be ready soon," Helena said, opening the refrigerator. Her English was better than it used to be, but it still sounded as though she felt the need to grip each word in her teeth and stretch it. She still spoke

Portuguese at home a lot, and on the phone with her friends, but Paulo knew that his dad didn't like it. It was one thing for him to bullshit with the guys at the club, it was another for his wife not even to *try* to learn, he said. He constantly said that English was the language that everyone has to understand, like it or not, all over the world.

Nuno shook his head, grabbed another can of beer, and went into the other room. "Hurry up," he called. "Hungry."

Helena turned her back to Paulo and hunched over the sink. They heard the pop and hiss of his beer opening.

"You know, he proud, Paulo." Helena smiled over her shoulder, her hands busy. "Proud of you."

Paulo knew his mom used to be pretty, with straight black hair that hung to her waist. It kind of shocked him when he first saw the pictures. When he was younger, he was fascinated by her eyes. "Why can't mine be like that?" he'd ask her, and she'd laugh and tell him that his were just as *belo*. Paulo used to sit on her lap and they'd look at old albums together. He didn't think his dad liked it though, because he'd usually go right outside when they were doing it, the screen door banging shut behind him.

She'd gained a lot of weight—she always blamed American food—and her ankles had grown swollen with arthritis. Her hair was mostly gray and it just kind of hung there. Paulo wasn't sure if she was still trying to dye it black. She used to leave the dye out in the bathroom until he told her the smell of it made him feel sick.

The year before, Helena had come to watch one of Paulo's junior varsity games, but as his dad drifted into the crowd to watch, his neck snapping away as cheers exploded across the street at the varsity field, she watched him from the car with the window open. Every once in a while Paulo could hear her shouting to him in Portuguese between cigarettes. After the game he saw Dane, one of their forwards, imitating her, calling out in gibberish to one of his friends. "Who the fuck *is* that?" he laughed.

Paulo wanted to strangle Dane. He wanted to kick him in the stomach while he was slumped down in the yellow grass and damp leaves. But he just stood there watching, and then he jogged over to their car, his heart pounding. But his mom hadn't heard. She kissed his cheek with dry lips and stubbed a cigarette out. "Good job, hon. Good job. You do good. You do very good."

That night Paulo fell asleep thinking about something different for once. He thought about how it would feel to really hurt Dane, to knock him out. To make him bleed. And the weird thing was that it didn't scare him at all.

· THURSDAY ·

"You didn't call me." Isabella usually wore her hair up in a bun, one stray strand dangling over her forehead, but today it was down around her shoulders. She wore skirts a lot, was a good student, and wanted to go to Boston College if she could get in. When Paulo met her again in the summer, he had vaguely remembered her from eighth grade. Back then she was quiet, had acne that reddened her face, and wore baggy sweaters. She was way hotter now.

"I couldn't."

"Whatever." She leaned in as if to kiss him and then pulled away at the last minute. She wouldn't say for sure that she was his girlfriend. Sometimes it pissed him off.

"Do you want to go to Jessie's on Friday?" Paulo still couldn't believe that *he* was going. But he tried to say it casually.

"Maybe I'll meet you there."

Paulo stared at her right front tooth. It was a bit discolored. He wondered if it was fake, but he'd never asked her.

"Do you care?"

"No," he lied, and leaned back against his locker.

"Stay after school tomorrow," she said.

"I have practice.

"Skip it."

"I can't."

Isabella chewed on her bottom lip. "Michelle asked me if we were going out."

"What'd you tell her?"

"She said everyone is starting to think we're together, so why don't I just say it."

"What'd you say?"

"She said she thinks we're good together, and we should, you know, do what we talked about."

"If you want," he said, trying to stay calm. Classes got out and suddenly students flooded the spaces around them.

"We can."

"We can?"

"Soon," she promised, looking down the crowded hallway. She took one step away. Paulo's eyes locked on the white sliver of skin above her jeans, where her shirt didn't quite reach. "I have class now."

"Soon," he repeated, "like when?" But she'd started off down the hall, and she didn't look back.

· FRIDAY ·

They were down in the dugouts. The smoke mixed with the mist that coated the field. The lights were off, and the carefully raked brown dirt shone in the moonlight. Paulo started getting high last year. This kid who lived down the street, Chris, got him into it. He played in a band.

"I'd fuck Ms. Sanderson," said Todd Last. He had been one of the stars of the team last year, along with Jessie. His hair was long and tucked behind his ears. Paulo thought about telling him about his pictures of Isabella, but he knew he shouldn't. Would they think it was weird? Or cool? Probably cool, Paulo thought, but he didn't want to risk it.

"Sure you would," snorted Tommy Motola, a short, stocky Italian kid who played defense. "Sure you would. Who wouldn't?"

They crumpled silver cans in their hands and picked off the tabs, flicking them at each other and out into the grass. The rumor was that if university security busted you, they'd hand you over to the Rhode Island State Police. They drank as quickly as they could, belching and spitting with each long sip.

Suddenly Todd crouched down. "Get down," he hissed, "someone's coming." Paulo crouched in the dirt and braced his hands against the cool stone wall, but his stomach shifted with the beer and the pizza they'd wolfed down and he farted.

Tommy stifled his laughter but it quickly began to escape as he gasped for breath. Todd started snickering too. "Fucking stinks," he said.

Paulo raised his head cautiously, sweat trickling down his back. There were people running across the field toward them. Were those black uniforms? The glint of a badge? The back of his head grew warm, as if a bubble had burst.

"Last? Motola? Why didn't you tell us you were coming here?"

It was only Nick and Jessie. Paulo looked back at Todd. Had he known the whole time?

"Who invited him?" asked Jessie, pointing toward Paulo.

"No clue," said Todd.

"Fuck off," Paulo said. He laughed weakly and wiped his hands on his jeans. "You did, Todd."

Todd shook his head and shared a grin with Jessie.

"Fuck it. Let's go to my house and call a bunch of people," Jessie said. "My parents finally left for the night."

"Do you jack off?" Isabella asked, wiping her mouth. Paulo eased onto his back in Jessie's parents' bed. It was three a.m. and mostly everyone was passed out. His parents thought he was staying at Todd's. "Good player," was all that Nuno had said, his head buried in the paper, when Paulo mentioned it.

"When we can't do this, do you?"

He sort of nodded.

"My older brother says every guy does it." She smirked. "So, what do you think about?"

"What?"

"What do you think of when you're doing it?" she repeated slowly.

"Why?"

Suddenly Isabella sprawled over him, reaching to the floor for something. Her hair dusted Paulo's face. The skin on her back was smooth.

"That's what the pictures are for," she said absently. "Right? So you'll always think of me. And I like when you do it, too. I like how it feels, like, to know."

"What are you doing?" he said, but he knew she was reaching for a condom. She had some in her purse; she'd showed him the other day. But when was he supposed to put it on? What if he wasn't good at it?

"Paulo, stand up." Isabella stood over him. Her shirt was off, her skin yellow in the light.

She was holding his camera and pointing it.

Paulo took the camera, relieved, and pretended to snap a picture.

"Wait!" whispered Isabella. They could both hear drunken voices and loud thumping in the hall. Paulo tossed her shirt to her and zipped his fly.

"No, hold on." Isabella found the lock on the door and then came back. "Paulo, take it," she said, biting her lip and staring at the ceiling dramatically. The thumping stopped.

He aimed. "Why do you like this so much?"

She shrugged. "You don't?"

"Take off your jeans."

"Not until you take a picture of me."

He raised the camera and hurriedly snapped a shot of her from the waist up. "More," she said. Then, in one fluid motion, she swept her underwear down and stepped out of them. "But not tonight," she whispered, "okay? Not tonight."

· SATURDAY ·

"Did you bring the camera?" she whispered.

But who would take the pictures? Paulo wasn't sure he could do both things at the same time. As they walked across the yard, he checked the driveway to see which car his parents had taken, so he'd know which car to be listening for. His hands were trembling as he unlocked the front door.

As they moved down the hallway, Isabella's hand was warm on the small of his back. Paulo wondered if she could feel him sweating.

He stopped. His bedroom door was closed, even though he always left it open. Isabella kissed the back of his neck and giggled. "Why are you stopping?"

He pointed at the door, puzzled, and Isabella shrank back, her smile fading. "Paulo, are you joking?" she whispered. "Is someone here?"

He pushed the door open and looked inside. The room was empty.

"There's no one here," he said. "It's okay."

"Why'd you scare me like that?" But Isabella was laughing, and as they walked in, she toyed with her shirt and then took it off. "Ta-da!" she said. She twirled around in a circle. How was she so relaxed?

Wait, were there noises coming from the other room? Paulo couldn't focus on her, and when he did, he didn't get the rush that he normally did.

"Come to bed," he said, because it seemed like the right thing to say. He knew it'd be fine once they got started. The satin of her bra was soft against his chest. Isabella wrapped her hands around his shoulders and kissed him.

But then he heard something again. A clicking. Or a creaking.

Isabella lay down on her back and tugged at his shirt, then pulled on his neck. When he resisted she scowled. "What? What's wrong?"

"Hold on," Paulo whispered.

He slipped out into the hallway. "Hello?" His voice sounded weird in the empty silence.

Isabella was silent. Or had she whispered something under her breath? Paulo peered in. She was crouched on the bed, yanking her shirt on.

"What *is* it?" she mouthed. "What the hell?" Her eyes flashed.

He held up one finger to tell her to wait and walked quietly down the hallway of the small house. He didn't see anything in the living room. There was no one in the kitchen. As he turned around and his eyes swept across the room, he breathed deeply and his mind accelerated. Back to his bedroom, close the door, lie down. Back to Isabella, her smooth skin, her hot breath.

Because she was so still, it took a second before Paulo could focus on the back of his mother's head, sticking up between the shelves crowded with books and framed pictures. She was sitting at the desk with her back to him, her gray hair striped with a few strands that were still dyed black.

"Mom? what are you doing?" He words poured out before he was ready. At the sound of his voice she whirled around, her white face flushing red.

"Paulo?" she said, too loudly. Why hadn't she gotten up when they came in? Why hadn't she said anything?

"Why aren't you at grandpa's?" His voice stuck in his throat, hoarse and angry. "What are you doing?"

Paulo stepped around the desk to see. Helena just sat there, motionless. She seemed frozen, and Paulo had to push by her legs to get around her. "Mom!" he said. "Move!"

Isabella could probably hear them. What was she doing in there?

Two cardboard boxes rested at Helena's feet. They were torn open. The pictures of Isabella, with some cards mixed in, were splayed out on the desk.

Paulo's mouth opened but nothing came out. The heat of a fever washed over him, and sweat blinked on his forehead. His eyes found the contours in the stained rug, the toes of his Converse.

Helena's eyes were wide and sad, staring directly at her son. Her fingers tapped the desk relentlessly, drumming in the quiet. It was as if the movements of her hand were out of her control.

They both listened to the footsteps breaking the silence, slapping down the hallway. It sounded as if Isabella stumbled at the end. Paulo squeezed his hands together tightly. He wanted to run after her. He wanted his mom to stop staring at him. He did nothing.

The screen door slammed. It seemed to awaken Helena, and when she raised her hand from the desk, a photograph stuck to it. She absently shook it off and pointed at Paulo. But she didn't say anything, and after a second, she dropped her hand to her lap.

Paulo had nothing to say to defend himself. He was a bad son. He was a pervert. He felt weightless, as if he could rise and drift away with the slightest breeze. Isabella was starting her car outside, but it seemed as though she were miles and miles away.

He turned toward the door. He would run outside and chase her. He'd run down the street if necessary, hitting the bumper with his hands, begging. Like they did in the movies. He'd try to fix this.

Instead, he stepped closer to the desk. His mother sat before him, mute, shaking her head very slightly. Isabella stared back at him from the desk, her eyes half closed, her head tilted back, her hands covering her breasts. It was one of his favorites. Paulo closed his eyes. *Why did she steal the boxes from under my bed? What the hell was she looking for?*

It didn't matter anymore. Helena eased off of the chair and scraped pictures and cards into neat piles, shuffling pieces of Isabella together with her hands.

Paulo was beginning to think he might get sick. One of the pictures had ripped. It was no good anymore. He'd throw it away. He watched his mom place all of the pictures back and cover the boxes. Then she motioned for him to sit next to her.

It was strange, she didn't really look angry. Her face kind of looked the way that it did in the early mornings, when Dad was singing in the shower and she'd just stand there wringing her hands as she watched Paulo eat.

"Are these yours?" she asked abruptly.

Paulo didn't say anything. A drop of sweat leaked from one of his armpits and tickled his side. He was a coward.

"Don't lie." Now she was the one to look down at the floor. "Did you even know they were here?"

Paulo shook his head. "No."

Helena closed her eyes and nodded as she took a deep breath. She looked as though she was either going to cry or scream, the way her bottom lip was shaking.

"Your dad, he sick." She coughed. "Sick. Very sick. Like this."

Paulo stared at her, trying to understand. His ears were ringing.

"He—he want me to see," she said numbly, and then she corrected herself and tried again. "He have me come back here, get a . . . card, baseball card for his dad. She shrugged her sunken shoulders. "So, he want me to see. This." She looked at Paulo and tried to smile. "*Wanted* me to see."

"Mom—"

"I'm sorry, Paulo," she said. He thought she was going to say more. But she didn't.

He sat there, frozen. He pictured Isabella speeding away, crying, embarrassed. Had he lost her? He thought of Dad and Grandpa sitting next to each other on Grandpa's sagging couch, watching the Red Sox or Sporting Lisbon play, drinking.

"See, your dad," she tried again, her voice evening out a little. "He—"

But she couldn't finish. Her hand began tapping the desk again, but it was slower now, more methodical. "I just sorry." Her chin rested on her chest, and her eyes were half closed. Her entire body seemed to deflate, and for the first time, to Paulo, she looked small.

"Don't tell him, okay honey? We work it out. I tell him."

He knew she wouldn't. He wrapped his arms around her and held the back of her head tightly

"It's all right, Mom," he said. "It's okay."

"He don't mean it," she mumbled into his shoulder. "He love us. He love you. He do."

"I know," Paulo said.

But he wasn't sure. He stared out the window as his mom wheezed into his chest. Her hair smelled like cigarettes. The street was empty of cars, and there were no children out playing. Autumn leaves the colors of lemons and oranges littered yards and driveways. The wind had stopped, and the trees were standing very still, as if they'd never been touched.

all he needed

Nuno was sixteen when he met Mateo, and seventeen when it happened. Mateo had drifted into Lagos from somewhere else—maybe Cascais, or Estoril—and to the locals, it was obvious that he wasn't born there. There were only two types of men in their small town: fishermen and footballers. Mateo was neither. Everyone said he was an *idiota,* a man who said little because he could not say more.

However, rumors began to lazily follow Mateo after he had lived in Lagos for a few years. Rumors that he was running around with married women, that he'd even had sex with some of the younger schoolgirls. Most of the men scoffed; some swore that Mateo was actually a woman himself; some even told stories of him coming onto them. However, when Mateo wandered by them, with that wan, stoned smile spread across his thin, pink lips, they pulled their wives or children a little closer to their sides.

When the town had its dances and *festas* and everyone came, Mateo would stand outside the crowd, hands in his pockets, staring absently at the couples that swung each other around and at the nodding men who plucked guitars. Every so often, one of the younger girls would dare another to run up to him and shout something, but they ran away, red-faced and shrieking, before Mateo could speak. The small boys were nastier, bent on imitating their fathers, sometimes throwing rocks at him from far away as their parents danced.

But none of it seemed to faze him. Mateo just grinned, his straight white teeth shining in the last sparks of sunlight. Nuno thought he looked ridiculous with his long hair, like a *maricas.*

But once, at the market, Nuno had overheard Helena talking to a friend about Mateo after he'd shuffled by.

"I feel *bad* for him," she'd whispered, covering her mouth with her hand and giggling. "He's kind of cute, in a weird way."

Nuno's body had stiffened and blood had pounded in his veins, but he hadn't told Helena he'd heard her. Instead, he'd tried to forget it had ever happened. There was nothing to worry about. Or was there? Nuno often passed Mateo on his way to the football field after school, and he always felt jittery when he saw him. There was something different about the way Mateo walked, the way his hips swung jauntily, almost in rhythm. His eyes, unblinking, gazed out searchingly, but Nuno looked away. He'd never even spoken to Mateo. He had no reason to. Mateo was not a man. He was a child.

—

Nuno and Helena had been inseparable for almost two months now. Although they hadn't slept together yet, at Nuno's insistence they'd done nearly everything else there was to do. Unlike many of the girls that Nuno had been with before, Helena was two years older than he. When he kissed her cheek or neck, her skin smelled not just of the scented lotions that the other girls wore, but something darker, salty and strong. And she had promised that if they stayed together long enough, they could have sex. Nuno hadn't done it yet, but his best friend Antonio had, and Nuno was sick of listening to him brag about it. But the thing that drew Nuno to Helena most were her eyes, and he remembered that she had been made fun of years ago at school. One eye was brownish green, and the other shone bright blue.

"Did that feel good?" Helena asked. They were lying in bed. Her head rested on his stomach.

"The best," Nuno said, his mouth full of the banana he was eating. "Want some?"

"Let's go to the ocean. You're tired from practice. You're not going to want to do anything else."

"I might," Nuno said, reaching and pinching her leg. "I might."

"I don't believe you," she said, standing and searching for her underwear.

Nuno flung them at her and she laughed at him. "Fine, let's go swimming," he said, yanking on his shorts as he lay on his back.

"I knew it!" Helena pulled her shorts on and laughed to herself. "I just knew it."

"Knew what?"

"That you didn't want to again. Or couldn't."

"I could."

"Fine. Then you didn't want to."

Nuno stood up and stretched. "Why is that the choice?"

"Because it is."

"Why?"

"Choose one."

"I didn't want to, then, I guess." Nuno shrugged. "Have it your way."

"Why not?" asked Helena as they walked down the stairs.

"This conversation should end," said Nuno, picking up his football and pretending to throw it at her. "Why not? Why? Twice is not good? Are you used to so much more?"

"Maybe."

"Yeah? With who?" Nuno bounced the ball on the floor, hard. "With *who?*"

At this Helena stopped at the door and whipped her head around. "What are you talking about? What's wrong with you?"

Nuno walked past her into the yard. Down the dirt road, there was a group of small boys throwing rocks at something in a tree. Beyond them, narrow, sandy paths overgrown with scrub brush led down to the water. He watched the boys shout encouragement to each other.

"What have you heard about me?" Helena asked calmly from behind him.

"Nothing," Nuno said, not turning around. But he *had* heard things. That was the problem. He'd heard rumors that she'd already had sex, last year, with an older footballer named Leonardo, who had since moved away to play in Lisbon. He'd heard that even now, Helena sometimes went to the beach with other men. Antonio had told him all of this the other day as they sat in his backyard smoking cigarettes. Nuno had gone silent. Probably none of it was true. Picturing Helena in the arms of an older man made him nervous. What if Helena wanted someone with more experience? What if he wasn't satisfying her?

"Nuno?" Helena asked sharply, a drop of sweat visible on her brow, her hands on her hips. But as he turned around, all Nuno could see was Mateo's blank toothy stare, his long fingers touching Helena's bare back and rubbing her breasts.

"Mateo?" Nuno said quietly, glaring into her eyes. To this day he did not know exactly what made him say it.

Helena stepped forward and slapped his face, the ring on her hand slicing his lip. Nuno tasted the warm squirt of blood before he felt it. Later, he would have a scar there, a small indented line to remind him of his wife.

—

The next day, Nuno found Antonio at the docks, where he was selling fish with his father. Nuno waved to Antonio's father, who was hosing off the boat, as they walked away. They lit cigarettes and took a side road back toward town, and Nuno told him what'd happened with Helena.

"Mateo's hard to figure out," Antonio said at one point. "I don't know what is true and what isn't. But I've heard tons of stories, Nuno. Even my dad, he said to be careful of him. He's not right in the head." He grinned. "But the women like him."

"Why would they?"

Antonio cast his cigarette butt away. "I don't know."

"I mean, how does he do it? He has some power over them or something? It's ridiculous."

"He fucks like a rabbit. Or he has a huge dick. I don't know."

Nuno scowled. He was enough for Helena, right?

"But the younger girls, Nuno? In school? It's not right. Someone should—"

"Young girls?" They turned right onto the town's main street, where it was more crowded, and Nuno lowered his voice. "Where's Mateo working now? Is he on a boat?"

Antonio rolled his eyes. "No, of course not! He's doing bitch's work, cleaning and cutting on the docks. They wouldn't let him go out."

Nuno thought about pointing out that that was mostly what Antonio did, but decided against it. Instead, he followed his friend into the market.

"Hey, Marcel!" Antonio said. He slapped hands with the owner and bought two bottles of beer, passing one to Nuno as they headed down to the beach. Sitting in the sand and watching the waves, Nuno drank quickly. He felt lightheaded, and couldn't stop thinking about Helena, and Mateo. It was as if they were connected now, even though he knew they weren't. Or he didn't think they were.

"Someone needs to teach that *filho da puta* a lesson."

Antonio smacked his lips and took another sip. "My dad said the same thing."

"Yeah?" Nuno's stomach growled. He was sick of talking about Mateo.

"Yeah, scare him or something. He needs a good talking to. He needs to have some respect."

"He needs a punch in the face," said Nuno.

"Why is he even here? Why Lagos?" Antonio finished his beer and threw it to the sand. He was getting agitated.

"I don't know." Nuno took the last warm sip, grimaced, and stood up. "I'm going home to eat, okay?"

Antonio stood slowly. "Nuno, what if you're right? What if he did do something with Helena?"

"I don't think—"

"I don't either but we don't know, right? And she got so angry . . ."

"No." Nuno chopped the air with his hand. He felt like punching Antonio in the face, not Mateo. He'd already decided that he'd been wrong. Helena wouldn't do that. "No. Absolutely not."

"Why don't we teach him a lesson?"

"I'm going." Nuno walked away, but his friend followed.

"Someone's got to, right? It'll be fun. We'll scare him a little. You know how happy people would be? You know how funny it would be?"

Nuno shook his head.

"Someone's got to do something, Nuno. You said it yourself! So why not us?"

"Because it's a stupid idea! Why get involved?"

"But you'd have such a story for Helena, Nuno."

Nuno stopped walking, his hands in his pockets. The wind blew off the ocean, the cooler air of the coming night. It *would* be something to tell Helena. He hadn't talked to her since yesterday. Maybe it would help fix things.

"We'd be heroes, Nuno."

"Maybe," Nuno said finally. "I've got to go home now, though."

"Think about it!" called Antonio. "See you tomorrow!"

On the walk home, Nuno wondered what his mother was cooking. He wondered if he'd see Helena tomorrow. He thought about her bare legs, and football, and how he needed to buy more cigarettes.

And he thought of Mateo. He couldn't help himself.

⚊

Two nights after he spoke to Antonio, Nuno sat in the backyard with his mother, Rosalita, as she tended to the firepit. Nuno's father, Justino, had come home early, which was a bad sign. He was in the house washing the smell of fish off of him, and as they waited for him, Rosalita mentioned Mateo.

"They say that he's been running around with some of the young girls!" she said to her son with wide eyes. "The pervert!"

Nuno sat silently before her, eating a piece of bread with some leftover *pasta de peixe*. He wondered, against his will, if his mother found Mateo attractive. Did all women?

"I'm almost glad I never had daughters," his mother said. "I wouldn't let them out of my sight!" She wagged her finger. "I wish he'd just go away."

Nuno nodded, spitting into the small fire. He had known since he was young that he could not have siblings. He remembered his mother trying to explain it to him years ago as he squirmed on her lap, Rosalita squeezing Nuno so hard that her chin pressed painfully against the top of his head.

"So quiet today!" Rosalita said. Then she looked at him closely. "What did you do to your lip?"

"Football." Nuno reached to touch the scab.

"And where's Helena? Will she come for dinner tonight, Nuno?"

Nuno's mother knew Helena from the outdoor market, with its stands packed with iridescent vegetables and tables steaming with vats of fish stew. Helena worked there after school. When his mother had seen them together a few times, she told Nuno that Helena was a good choice, and that he should start thinking about marriage.

Nuno leaned back and chewed, imagining his mother hearing what Antonio had said about Helena and Mateo. "She can't come," he lied. "She's working."

"At the market? No she's not! I saw her mother this morning. She has no plans tonight. I already asked. Go call on her, Nuno, bring her for dinner. Your father will be out soon."

The breeze smelled of salt and red wine. There was nothing else to do. Nuno walked down the street to Helena's, shaking the breadcrumbs from his shirt. He toyed with his lip. It hurt to touch it, but his finger was drawn there. He hadn't seen Helena since it happened, but his mother didn't know that. She'd been avoiding him. He trusted Helena, he did. But he couldn't stop thinking about it. And what about the way she reacted when he asked about Mateo? What did that mean? That she was outraged because what he said was so insane? Or, she was outraged because, well, because he'd found out the truth? It couldn't be. Could it?

Nuno blinked and swept the dirt road with his eyes: the small white houses packed tightly on each side, the bright green brush mixed with wildflowers, the palm trees that spilled into small yards with hammocks strung up. If he saw Mateo now he honestly didn't know what he would do.

"Helena?" Nuno called to the closed front door of her house, the tiny balcony where clothes flapped on a taut line. There was only silence, the chirping of birds, the cheers of children playing football at the end of the road. "Helena!" he called again, and then stepped inside. Her father would be fishing; it was rare to be home now, as Nuno's father was. Her mother was at the market. Helena, he guessed, could be at the beach with her friends, or visiting her mother.

Her bedroom was closed. Nuno paused outside, staying perfectly still. This was stupid. What was he doing? But he couldn't help it. He put his ear to the door and strained to hear something. Anything. Was that—was that a moan he heard? Or was that the wind?

Finally, he swallowed and shoved the door open.

Nothing. There was a cotton dress folded on the bed. Nuno touched the fabric. He had never seen her wear it before. He walked over to stand by the window, watching the children outside run in circles, fighting for the ball like animals. One child was already ahead of the rest, and the way he shielded the ball and fended the others off with quick jabs of his small shoulders reminded Nuno of himself.

Nuno found himself anxiously looking out for Mateo's smiling face. And where was Helena? He jogged to the market, but she wasn't there, and he knew his parents were waiting for him. On the way home, he thought some more about what Antonio said. Mateo could use a good scare, he thought. Maybe that would get him out of Nuno's head once and for all, and Helena and he could go back to the way things used to be. Maybe if they scared him enough, he'd leave Lagos. Then, they could tell everyone. They *would* be heroes.

Maybe Antonio wasn't such an *idiota*, after all.

———

Nuno awoke with a start at two a.m., hearing his name being called softly. For a few seconds he lay there, not wanting to acknowledge the hoarse whisper, unable to even consider rising from the web of cotton blankets wrapped around him. In that brief instant, he called it all off. He apologized for even thinking it. He begged himself to go back to sleep, to the dreams unspoiled by Mateo's long fingers and unceasing grin.

"Nuno!" Antonio coughed. Nuno smelled tobacco. "Wake up! We don't have much time."

Nuno turned on his side and opened his eyes. On the night table was Helena's drawing of Nuno playing football. He picked it up and noticed how wrinkled it was. The edge was ripped. He hadn't wanted it at first, but she had looked so proud when she gave it to him that he had to take it. And he did like it—the way she'd exaggerated his muscles, the way his leg was cocked back behind the ball, ready to shoot.

"Nuno, what the hell? Get up! What are you doing?"

Nuno put the picture down. "Shhh!" he whispered. "You're gonna wake up my parents. Let's do it another night. I'm tired."

"No!" Antonio rapped on the window. "Tonight! We're doing it tonight! That's the plan! What're you, scared? Get up or I *will* wake up your parents!" He knocked on the window again for emphasis.

Nuno groaned and sat up. "Fine!" he hissed. "Go wait for me in the street. Go!"

When Antonio was gone, Nuno sat there for another minute, rubbing his eyes. A cool breeze drifted in, and he shivered. Why had he ever thought this was a good idea?

Oh well. He was up now. And his mind was racing. He wouldn't be able to get back to sleep.

Nuno and Antonio lay on their stomachs in the sand under one of the unused docks. The tide was creeping up the beach toward them. This was the spot they'd chosen to begin at, so they could first check to see if anyone else was on the beach. If anything went wrong after this, they'd agreed to meet in Nuno's backyard. It had been fun putting the plan together, drinking beers and rehearsing what they would do. This wasn't fun. The sand was damp and cold and Antonio's breath smelled like liquor, but he hadn't offered Nuno any. The whole thing felt stupid and juvenile.

Mateo's shack was sunk down between two dunes, behind the skeletons of old beached boats that were slowly being stripped of wood and metal. In the white light of the moon, as they crawled toward the door, Nuno noticed that beside the shack, there was a canoe flipped upside down and covered in blankets. Antonio elbowed him and nodded.

"That's probably where it happens, Nuno."

In front of the shack Mateo had laid thin, painted pieces of wood to form a makeshift deck. Nuno noticed a broom leaning against the house, and next to it a neat pile of white shells and rocks.

Nuno pressed his hand lightly against the door, and his stomach suddenly tightened. "Hey, wait," he whispered, "what if he's not alone?"

Antonio slid a knife from his pocket and jabbed the air. "Then you've saved the girl, Nuno," he said loudly. "Then you're a goddamn hero."

"What the hell is that?" Nuno pointed to the knife.

"What?"

"Why do you have that? We're just—"

"Oh, stop being a baby, Nuno! It's for protection. That's all."

Nuno punched his friend in the shoulder. *"Estúpido!"*

"Cale-se!" Antonio put a finger to his lips. "Let's go."

Nuno shoved the door and it dragged against the wooden floor. Antonio's breath itched on the back of his neck. The dark room smelled strangely sweet, and Nuno waited for his eyes to adjust. To the right, under a small rectangular window, was the bed. Next to it, a lantern burned.

What was he supposed to do? They hadn't been able to rehearse this part. *Just scare him,* Antonio kept saying. Okay, how? Nuno looked back at Antonio and shrugged. Antonio stood in the doorway. He looked stunned.

"This is stupid," Nuno said. "Let's just go."

But Antonio snapped out of it, and glared disdainfully at Nuno. *"Filho da puta,"* he said, and jabbed Nuno in the chest. Then he took three careful steps, until he was standing over Mateo. He motioned for Nuno to open the door a little more so he could see.

"So, you like our women, do you?" Antonio said.

Mateo lay on his back, his mouth open. His hands were folded across his chest.

"We want you out, okay? Out of Lagos. Out!"

Mateo stirred a little at this, then turned on his side, away from them.

"You hear me?" Antonio raised his voice and kicked the bed.

Nuno's stomach pitched wildly. "Enough!" he said. "Enough!"

Mateo sat up and almost fell off the bed. "Who's there? Hello?" He looked small in the darkness. Nuno shrank back against the door and tried to hide in the shadows. He could just run away right now, he thought. Screw Antonio. He could pump his legs down the shore and not stop until he was far, far away.

"Is that you?" Mateo whispered, standing and rubbing his eyes. Then he saw Antonio. And he screamed.

Antonio launched himself at him, covering his mouth and wrapping an arm around his neck. "Nuno, help!" he demanded.

Nuno couldn't move.

Antonio wrestled Mateo toward the door, with Mateo's elbows and legs flailing at him. "Ow! He bit my hand, this *caralho*! He bit my hand! *Foda-se!*"

They pushed out through the door and fell to the sand, Mateo squirming under Antonio, who overpowered him easily and pulled his arms behind his back.

"Cale-se!" he shouted. "And we won't hurt you. Nuno, get the fuck over here! Nuno!"

Nuno ran over and grabbed Antonio's shoulders. "Stop!" he said. "Enough!"

But Antonio's eyes blazed. He jerked away from Nuno and pressed his knees into Mateo's back. "My friend Nuno has something to tell you, *cabrão*." He looked at Nuno and smiled. "Tell him!"

But Nuno just stared out at the waves.

"Tell him! Tell him to stay away from Helena!"

Mateo squirmed more at this, and managed to turn his head around. His face was barely visible in the dark. "Helena, that *puta*," he said, spitting out sand. *"Puta,"* he said again, twisting away from Antonio's grasp.

"Cabrão!" cried Nuno, and grabbed Mateo's head, slamming it into the sand. *"Foda-se!"*

"Yes!" shouted Antonio gleefully.

Mateo snorted and spit, and Nuno drove his face into the sand again.

"My turn!" crowed Antonio. "Nuno, hold him!"

Mateo pitched back and forth wildly, but Nuno held fast. Antonio held Mateo's face down in the sand, and he sputtered and kicked his feet. The waves were coming closer, licking at the sand right near them. Nuno suddenly felt alive, as alive as he did when he flew down the field pushing the ball, the hum of the crowd lightning up his spine.

"Okay, it's enough," Nuno said, letting up on Mateo a little. He wasn't struggling anymore. Antonio was still pressing Mateo's face into the sand. He leaned in so that he was talking right into his ear. "Get out of here. And don't ever, ever say anything like that again."

Nuno let go and stood up. Mateo didn't move. One of his arms twitched violently.

Antonio wound up and kicked Mateo in the side. "That's for my sister," he said.

But now, the thoughts were coming, unabated. Mateo had said Helena's name. Did he know *of* her, or did he know her?

"Let's put him back and go," Antonio said. "Help me."

Nuno eased off and stood up. His head was swimming. Mateo just lay there, recovering. Antonio kicked at the sand near his head.

"Get up!" he said. "Hey, Nuno, lets just leave him here."

Nuno nodded. He wanted to ask Mateo what he knew. He wanted to ask about Helena. To get this settled once and for all.

"Hey, Mateo," Nuno said roughly, leaning down. "Hey. Get up."

But he didn't move.

Antonio kicked him in the side. "Nuno, outta the way."

"Stop!" Nuno said. Mateo's face was still stuck in the sand. "I think we knocked him out," he said. "We should—"

But what would they do? Drag him inside and leave him? Wait for him to wake up? They could put cold water on his face. *But what if he didn't wake up?* Was he breathing? He was talking and swearing and spitting just a second ago, wasn't he?

"How hard did you kick him?" Nuno said. His mouth was dry and it was hard to get the words out. "Why—"

"Nuno! Someone's coming!"

Nuno turned and could make out a distant figure walking down the beach.

"Get him inside! Grab his arms!" They hurriedly heaved Mateo up and half-dragged him through the door and to his bed. He didn't move a muscle. He didn't make a sound. They dropped him onto the bed and he rolled onto his side toward the wall. Sand sprayed all over his pillow.

"Leave him! Let's go!" shouted Antonio.

"We can't!" Nuno was shaking. He ran to the door and peeked out. The figure was much closer now, coming up the shore toward them. It was a woman, and her dress shone white in the moonlight. She'd probably heard everything.

"Antonio! We have to—"

"I'm gonna run!" Antonio fired back, and pushed by Nuno. "Let's go! Let's go! We can make it!"

Nuno stood there, paralyzed.

"Nuno, he'll be fine! Let's go!" He punched Nuno in the chest. "Run!"

With that, Antonio took off running. He faded quickly into the night, the crashing of the waves and the hum of the wind.

Nuno was alone. He went and stood over Mateo. The candlelight flickered across his face. Mateo wasn't breathing. One arm was extended limply, and his hand was bent back against the wall.

Nuno pressed his hands against his chest, pushing. He felt nothing. "Wake up," he said. "Wake up, wake up." There was a numbness spreading through his body. He reached out and tried to pull Mateo's hand away from the wall, but it just fell back. His skin was warm.

Then he remembered, and ran to the door. The woman was about fifty yards away, walking purposefully through the dark night. Was she coming here? Nuno couldn't take the chance. He slipped outside and made his way to the side of the shack, ducking under a window, and sank to his stomach.

When she got close enough, Nuno's heart fluttered and then stopped. He recognized the loping way that she walked. He knew the habit that she had of flicking her hair away from her face with her right hand. Keeping her head angled down.

Nuno watched through the window as Helena opened the door and glided in. His eyes followed her as she knelt down next to the bed and placed a hand on Mateo's shoulder. Her head leaned toward his, her hair grazing his face. She whispered something, and brushed sand off the covers.

After about a minute, he saw her step back, frightened. "Mateo?" he thought he heard her say. "Mateo?" Then she put one knee on the bed and reached to touch his chest. After a few seconds, she put her head against his heart. Then her entire body stiffened, and she yanked her hand away.

Helena wrapped her arms around herself and spun around in place, her dress swirling around her. She ran to the door, looked out, and then collapsed to the floor next to the bed. Even outside the house, even with the looming crash of the waves, Nuno could hear her begin to wail.

He leaned against the wall and wondered when he would wake up, curled in his bed at home. When this would be over. Above him, the stars blinked on and off. The sky was clear. Antonio was gone. Mateo was gone. And only Helena was left, shuddering in the darkness, all alone.

Nuno waited for Helena to run away, or scream. When she didn't, he crept away from the shack, checking back over his shoulder to see if she'd seen him. When he was sure she hadn't, he walked aimlessly down the shore for miles, until his feet were cold and numb.

When dawn finally broke, Nuno tried to focus his eyes, but everything was spinning away from him. The fog, like silver smoke. The orange sun, climbing the Eastern sky. When he was far away from everything he knew, he stripped off his clothes and left them in the dunes. Then, he rinsed his hands in the shallow swells, examining them closely, as if for the first time. When he was ready, he pushed out deep, feeling the sun warm his back as he swam.

one last thing

Like a child, he couldn't sit still. But he looked into her eyes until she was the one to look away, as if it was the least he could do.

"Catarina, your father died yesterday. In Lisbon. At the hotel."

Looking back, she thought she would have shaken her head. But she nodded instead. She could not understand why.

"Where is he now?" she asked.

Rui blinked. "Where is he," he repeated softly, "where? I don't know. They will bring him back here for the funeral. But you, what about you? Are you okay? Come here." He reached out across the table for her hand but she flinched and rose, weightless suddenly, and glided through the screen door, the rusty squeak echoing in her mind. She stood on the front lawn where the grass was brown in patches and prickled her bare feet, listening to the faint cries of children playing down near the ocean at Praia de Adraga.

Catarina knew her cousin was watching her from the doorway. She stayed as still as she could and watched the clouds drift across the tops of the green mountains in the distance. They were moving very quickly. Her father was gone. He would not be back tomorrow, and she would not cook dinner for him again. Her stomach tightened suddenly and she put her hand on it, wondering if this was what it felt like to be pregnant. Wondering if she was going to be sick. What had she said to him as she helped him up the stairs to the train? He had asked her again to come with him. His white hair was combed neatly to the side, and he was dressed in the heavy gray suit that he always wore on his trips to the city. It was the only suit he owned. *Had* owned, she thought. The only suit he *had* owned.

"Have a safe trip, Daddy," she'd said, kissing him goodbye.

The lines around his eyes deepened. "You sure you won't come, my love? We will find a husband for you in Lisbon."

She shook her head. "And a wife for yourself," she said. Then she laughed and waved goodbye.

"Catarina, come inside." Rui was still standing behind her, but she did not turn around. The sun was warm on her face now, her chest. She closed her eyes. It was a strange idea, that those were the last words he would ever hear her say. She felt as though she was holding her breath and could not let it go. What was the last thing that she'd said to her mother the day before she disappeared so many years ago?

"Catarina, I'm going on a trip." Her mother had been sitting at the table, drinking red wine before Catarina's father returned from work.

Catarina was six years old. "Where?" she asked. "When?"

"I'll come back soon," her mother sniffled. "I just need to go."

"With Daddy?"

"No, he needs to stay here. But you could come with me," her mother whispered, "and we'd see Daddy soon?"

Catarina could hear her father's car pulling into the driveway.

"Okay," she said, "but let's come back soon."

"I'll come for you tomorrow morning, early," said her mother. "Don't tell Daddy."

Catarina didn't tell, but her mother never came. Her father locked himself in his room for five days while Rui's mother cooked and looked after Catarina. She came home from school after a week to find her father waiting for her in the driveway. He picked her up and swung her around.

"You are the head of the house now," he said. "You, my angel, will look after me as I look after you." He hugged her so hard that it hurt.

As Catarina grew up, the rumor that sighed and whispered its way through the family was that her mother had flown to America. They had cousins there, in Rhode Island. She was a dancer, an airline stewardess, a poet. No one knew for sure, and no one knew why she left when she had so much—a small but beautiful house near the water in Sintra, a loving husband, and a young daughter.

Catarina finally turned away from the mountains. Her cousin had gone back inside, and she found him sitting at the table thumbing through a stack of papers. He licked his finger and then handed one to her as she sat down.

"When you're ready, we can talk about the house, and the money he left. There's not too much." Rui cleared his throat. "But it's all for you."

"I'm ready," she said. Her mind was racing. She felt young and old all at once, as if she were glued to her seat but also free. Everything she touched felt alive. The printed numbers on the page in her hand shivered. She let it flutter to the floor.

As she prepared to leave over the next few weeks, she sometimes felt it was her destiny to be going to the States. Everything might have happened for a reason. She never told anyone, but sometimes she couldn't help but wonder if she would see her mother. Catarina swore to herself that she would not seek her out, would not ask about her, would not even think about her. She would be completely alone in her new life. The idea excited her, and in these moments she felt a great sense of clarity. When she looked into the mirror, she could see her future.

At other times she missed her father terribly. His clothes were strewn about the house, and she couldn't bring herself to touch them. One afternoon she pillaged the drawers to his room, tears jerking down her cheeks as she rummaged through his belongings. She expected, somehow, to find letters from her mother, or evidence of a secret, more fulfilling life. But the only thing she found that he had hidden was the deed to their house and an envelope of *escudos* that he must've forgotten about many years ago. Catarina folded the yellowed and brittle cash carefully, and tucked it into her pocket.

At the funeral she told of the last words spoken between them. Her cousins from Cascais, his friends from Lisbon, and more than half of the small town laughed somberly. Afterward her house was full of fresh flowers and food wrapped in foil.

She did not tell her plans to anyone but Rui, who was twenty-seven, five years younger than she was, and he helped her arrange for a passport, a visa, a flight. He had been to the States many times in the past, had visited Rhode Island and even New York City. Finding family there had been hard, he warned her, and it would be even more difficult now. Catarina told him that she didn't care. So Rui spent hours on the phone trying to find her a place to live while she sat next to him silently and listened. At her request, Rui also gave her English lessons, teaching her simple words and phrases that she turned over and over in her mouth awkwardly. In exchange, Catarina cooked him dinner, using the skills she perfected as chef at the best restaurant in town, Alcobaca.

The time to leave grew closer. Somehow, word of her journey had leaked out to a few people. There were warnings from old friends, and cards sent professing sympathy and encouragement. It was not the way she wanted it. She wanted to simply disappear.

One night, as Rui wrote out flash cards for her, he asked how long she planned to stay in the States. She hesitated and he frowned. "You think you are lonely here," he said, "just wait."

"I don't know, a year or so at least?" she said finally, nonchalantly. But inside she seethed. She pictured streets full of flashing headlights, a new house with glimmering countertops, silver skyscrapers that punctured blue sky. Sometimes, she even felt that she was not alone in these visions of the future. Sometimes, someone was next to her.

Catarina was thirty-two and unmarried. She couldn't decide if it was because she had never met anyone she would even consider marrying, or if she simply didn't want to marry. She did enjoy her beauty; she found it useful. And there had always been men, the earliest brought to the house for dinner by her father—victims, as they drank and chewed, of those hopeful awkward silences that she coveted. She had chosen one from time to time, but they had never really moved her, never worked right. She found reasons to reject them, one by one. She preferred being by herself, especially in the morning when the sun shone through her window and warmed her bare feet in bed. One man had stuck around for a while; he was an architect who tied his hair into a long ponytail with a silver elastic. He seemed similar to her at first: he didn't really care, he didn't need her. They existed separately and together, regardless. But in the mornings he acted like a child, pushing against her and pleading for her warm body. Regardless of whether she gave in or not, it struck her as weak, and soon she was finished with him.

So Catarina lived with her father, cooked for him, and kept him company. And although he admitted often that it upset him that she was still alone, Catarina knew that he was better off with her there. She told herself she always would be there for him, no matter what. He deserved it.

There was no one to worry about saying goodbye to. Her family was scattered throughout the country. She had never really known her mother's side. But she went over to Rui's house for dinner before she left. From the deck they watched the dogs run ragged circles in the grass. It had rained the night before and the smell of salt from the ocean was particularly strong. It was her first time seeing Uncle Armando after the funeral. He raised his wine glass and toasted her, but his eyes looked half closed.

"Your father always wanted you to marry," he said. "Not to go away alone."

"Maybe I take after my mother," Catarina said. The food steamed on the table. Aunt Carmen took her seat and raised her hands to pray. "Such a pretty girl, always," she said, bowing her head.

"May God bless you on your trip," said her uncle. He looked at Carmen and sighed. Across the table, Rui drank his entire glass of wine.

﹉

Catarina sat before the television and waited for her dinner to finish heating. She had cooked two nights ago, but there was so much left that she could eat for weeks by herself. She would see if Helena wanted any.

She could only tolerate the game shows on television, because it was easier to understand what was happening. But she was learning, little by little. And Helena was constantly teaching her new words, pointing with her plump hands to random objects. "Dishtowel," she would say, flapping it in the air and pointing, "microwave."

It was the middle of July, and Catarina had been in Rhode Island for one month. On the plane she had rapidly drunk the wine they gave her and then paid for two tiny bottles of Dewar's Scotch, which she mixed with water. When they shut the lights, she covered herself in a thin blanket and stayed awake, watching the plane inch forward on the map on the glowing screen in front of her, unwilling to believe what was happening. In the morning she watched, numb, as the gray city of Boston came into focus through the window.

Manny picked her up at Logan Airport and they drove south, down to a town near the ocean called Narragansett. He was an old friend of her cousin Alberto, who, he explained, used to live in Rhode Island but had long since moved to Florida, wherever that was. Manny owned a Portuguese restaurant and he spoke English, albeit poorly. For now, Catarina would stay at a house that Manny's friend owned, and pay him with the money she made working at his restaurant. She could also use Manny's spare Chevrolet pickup truck for a while if she kept it in good shape and paid for gas. All in all, between being paid under the table and her small inheritance, she'd be comfortable.

"You might want to wait until you adjust a little before starting work," Manny had said, his hand settling lightly on her back. He was a few years older, his thick black beard streaked with gray. His wife had divorced him ten years ago and moved to New Hampshire. He had told her this immediately, as they walked through the sliding doors of the airport exit. Then he lit a cigarette, sucked greedily, and offered her one. She had never smoked, and refused.

She liked the house well enough. It was not what she had pictured at all. The bottom floor was dusty and the couch sagged. There were seashells on the windowsills and dirty ashtrays on the tables. But the entire second floor was open and empty, as if it had been waiting for her. When Manny finally dropped her off, he stood in the driveway and nodded as she slung her bag over her shoulder and pushed her hair back.

"You gonna be all right here all by yourself?"

She nodded and leaned in to kiss him on the cheek. *"Obrigada,"* she said. "I will come to work Monday."

"Jeez, make it Tuesday," he said, his hand grazing her hip as she pulled away. For a second he looked uncertain. In English he muttered, "Monday is a throwaway. I don't need two cooks."

Catarina watched him drive away. Then she slowly walked around the house. Wildflowers had grown around the edges of the small yard, mixed with weeds and clover. When she stepped inside and closed the door behind her, her heart pounded. She was alone. The possibilities were endless, inviting. The silence rang in her ears.

Catarina met Helena the next day. She awoke and immediately walked out to the backyard, longing for the deck at their house in Sintra, the gentle hissing of the waves in the morning. But that world seemed far away, and she wondered if the space that she had created when she left had already been filled in. Somewhere in the neighborhood a lawnmower sputtered and came to life, and as Catarina turned to walk back inside she heard a door slam.

A large woman with dyed hair, wearing a blue dress and sneakers, waved to her, motioning her over. In a few minutes they were gleefully speaking Portuguese, their words firing in long, excited bursts as they sat next to each other in the shade. That night Catarina opened her door to find Helena waiting for her with ten different Tupperware containers filled with her cooking.

Almost every day after that, when Helena's husband Nuno went to the Lusitania Club to drink and watch soccer, Helena would call on her, and the two women would drink iced tea or a glass of wine and talk. Catarina told herself at first that she was humoring the old woman, but soon realized that she was the one who looked forward to her visits the most. Sometimes at work, her clothes sticking to her in the cloudy heat of the ovens, her hands peeling shrimp or stirring soup, she would remember something that Helena had said.

"But why does your husband never come over?" Catarina asked once as they sat in her kitchen. Helena had brought over pictures from when she was a girl in Lagos. "Such a cute man, I've seen him out in the garden, but I still haven't met him." Catarina had actually seen him a number of times, often staring sheepishly at her, a short man with a thick chest and longish gray hair. She thought he looked a bit like her father, and once she had waved, but he turned abruptly away.

Helena shook her head. *"Ele é tímido,"* she said. "Maybe one day he visit." She hesitated and then leaned back in her chair. Catarina stared at the way her dress stuck to her back, the streaks that the black dye left in her gray hair. "Maybe he is scared of you," Helena said. She burst out laughing, slapping her knee with her hand. "Maybe you are too beautiful for him!"

Catarina laughed. Last night she had sat at the restaurant bar after they were closed, let Manny fill and refill her glass. She let him rest his damp hand on her knee for a few minutes, but pulled away when he tried to kiss her goodnight outside. He shook his head and winced. "Sorry," he said, "sorry."

Helena was once again reciting the reasons that she would be dead soon. "My lungs," she said, "my weight, my legs, my back." She groaned and then coughed, rasping, the veins in her forehead and temples jumping. "When I die I'm going straight to Lagos. Sit on *a praia, nadar no oceano*. Nuno taught me to swim in Lagos many, many years ago. We were happier, you know? He was different back then." Catarina nodded and looked out the window. Helena had told the story more than once. "It wasn't like it is today! Look at you, so beautiful but alone, Catarina, all alone!"

Catarina had told Helena that her father had died recently and that her mother had left when she was young. Helena's response was to stand shakily and bang her fist on the table. "That's why you need a man!" she shouted. Sometimes her voice grew uncontrollably loud.

Catarina laughed at this pronouncement. "Well, *avó*, find me one," she said.

"Oh, if my Paulo wasn't married!" she said once. "Maybe he has a friend! I'll ask him."

But Catarina had seen Paulo when he came to visit, pulling his silver truck abruptly into the driveway in a cloud of dust and pebbles. She immediately knew what kind of man he was. He did not wait for his wife to get out of the car but strutted to the door, calling out for his father. Often the two men stood outside alone, Paulo motioning violently with his hands, Nuno standing with his hands in his pockets, looking down at the grass.

When she wasn't working, Catarina took day trips to different beaches, tanning in the sun, feeling men's eyes graze her body from time to time. She cooked and listened to the radio she had purchased, drinking wine as the summer sun set over the rows of houses each night, listening to the hum of mosquitoes or the distant screech of tires. Some mornings when she awoke, she felt as though no one in the world knew where she was, and it jolted her. She wasn't old, she thought. Helena was old. She could still be young and wild, just look at what she had done, leaving home. Maybe she would drive to Boston, New York, even California. She could do anything.

Other times, falling asleep, she asked herself why she had come here, why she stayed here. Her cousins weren't even here, only Manny with his drooping mustache and beard and tired eyes. He would do anything for her. Lying in her queen-sized bed in the silence of her house, the lone streetlight outside shining yellow through the open windows, she felt older than Helena, older than her father had been, and she wondered where she would die.

⁀

Catarina was in her bedroom, getting ready for her sixth week of work, when she thought she noticed something. She had never bought blinds; in fact, she avoided many simple errands because they'd proved more difficult than she'd imagined. When she went out for something she needed alone, her encounters were reduced to hopeless hand gestures and the nodding and shaking of heads. She made an effort, at first. But most people didn't—they just walked away and left her alone. If it was essential, then Manny or Helena would help. But she'd grown used to the bare windows, and enjoyed the light that poured in to wake her in the mornings, the moonlight that shone through at night. But now, standing there dripping, a refreshing shiver running through her after a cold shower, she thought she felt something. Did she feel it or see it?

She peered across the yard. It seemed strange that the blinds to Helena's bathroom window were down, because the rest of the windows were open. She could smell fish frying, Helena was cooking lunch. She let her towel drop and pulled on a pair of underwear and a bra quickly, jerking up the straps.

The bottom of the blinds inched up. She squinted in the stuffy haze of summer. Now there were a few inches between the windowsill and the blinds. If she could see the window so well, and if someone was there, they could see her. She slowly stepped to the side, her stomach a little queasy. She was out of sight now. Catarina craned her neck and watched as the blinds lifted a bit more. Below them all she could see was darkness, but as she sat on the bed to brush her hair she thought of how Nuno's face reddened whenever he saw her.

Catarina stood before the window and began brushing her hair. The breeze came through the screen softly and dried her skin. She had left the radio on downstairs, and a song that she recognized came on. American music, she had decided, was disorganized and beautiful, like graffiti on city streets. It was nothing like the careful plucking of *fado* that her father had listened to each night.

Suddenly, Catarina felt a pair of eyes alight on her and run down her legs and across her arms, as fast as the wind, as faint as the music. Her whole body tingled for a moment.

The blinds suddenly came down with a snap. She heard Helena's voice calling for her husband to come to the table.

Catarina quickly dressed. On the way to work, she decided that she could not be sure of anything. She also could not be blamed for anything. She pulled into the restaurant in a satisfying cloud of dust.

Three days later, on the first Saturday in August, Helena died. Catarina had worked a lunch shift but left early when not many customers showed, promising Manny she would be back to set up for dinner. He had grown more persistent with her lately, his face soft and defeated as he sat nursing a glass of wine or whiskey at the bar. He asked her to stay and drink with him after each shift, but she rarely did anymore, preferring to drive home, speeding in the night air, singing along with the blaring radio as she shifted gears. She knew he would keep waiting for her. When she did stay, she indulged him, sat close to him at the bar, watched him grow flustered and shaky as she giggled and poked his arm.

It was three p.m. There was an ambulance in front of Helena's house, the lights flashing silently. Further down the street, two teenage boys were playing Frisbee. Catarina walked across the yard and stood on the front steps, peering inside. Nuno sat at the kitchen table with his back to her, his head in his hands. Just as she was about to knock, a young man with blond hair tapped her on the shoulder.

"Are you family?" he asked quietly.

She turned and looked at him. He was biting his bottom lip.

"No?" she said, because she thought she understood, and then followed him as he walked to the ambulance.

"He doesn't want to come to the hospital," the man said quickly, pointing inside. "He told me to just take her away. Are you a friend?"

Catarina stared at him. "Friend," she said.

"You may be in shock," he said, and he touched the side of her shoulder. Catarina nodded and then shook her head, to cover herself both ways. The man looked puzzled. Catarina walked over to the ambulance and looked inside. She could see the large heap that was Helena covered in a blanket.

"Hey, Freddy!" called a man from the front seat. "You ready?"

"I'm sorry. She's gone," said Freddy, standing behind Catarina now. "We need to take her away. Tell her husband we will be in touch concerning the, um, arrangements for everything. Or he can call the hospital."

Catarina nodded, this time sure of herself. She couldn't remember the last thing that Helena had said to her. She wondered if Helena was in Lagos now. She wanted to believe that she was, but somehow she couldn't.

As the ambulance pulled away, Catarina walked back up the steps to the front door. It was still open, and Nuno was still seated at the table. He was breathing deeply, almost as if he were snoring. Catarina stood in the doorway and watched him for a while, wondering what she should do.

"Nuno," she said. "Nuno?"

He raised his head and turned around. His nose was wet and red. He waved her away.

Over the next few days she kept her eye on him. The driveway filled with cars. She watched people file in and out wearing stiff, dark clothes and carrying flowers. She did not go to the funeral, and she wondered whether Nuno had even known that she and Helena were such good friends. At night she strained to hear the familiar hum of visitors' voices speaking Portuguese across the yard, standing at the window with her ears against the screen.

And she let him watch her. It started almost immediately, and now it was more obvious; the way the blinds rustled as she moved from room to room in the mornings, the way the windows remained open. Catarina thought once she even saw his eyes, gaping and sad, framed with lines. But that was probably just in her head.

Standing there, day after day, letting the sunlight warm her, Catarina felt Nuno devour every piece of her as she undressed. She stood at the window bare-chested, brushing her hair, or let her towel drop as she danced to music from the radio. The blinds that she'd eventually bought remained in a heap of plastic bags in the hallway. She liked the fact that when Nuno came home from the club, he tried to force himself to walk slowly to his front door, to hide his excitement. Catarina could see it in the tightened way he moved, though; she could feel his pent-up anticipation. She'd been shocked, at first, then saddened by the whole thing. But then she'd found herself amused. There was nothing wrong with it, she thought. *Let him stare,* she thought boldly. *Maybe it was what he needed.*

She even brought her arm up to wave to Nuno once, standing naked in her bedroom window at dusk, the white light from her lamp shining on her olive skin. But she worried about his heart. So she kept her arm down and slowly turned around, so that he could see all of her.

fireflies

MATEO · 1941

You were the first one to speak to me, Helena. It was my ninth day here. The girls were taking a while to come around, but I knew it would happen eventually. I wasn't worried. They either feel sorry for me, or they want to piss off their boyfriends or husbands. Sometimes, they just want the attention. I have the gift, the spark, what do you call this? It runs in the men in my family; we all have this *capacidade especial.*

But you were different. You resisted. It took weeks for me to convince you to just spend time with me, and it was months, even, before you would come to visit me after sundown. Even on that first night, you sat far away from me, gazing out at the sea. When I tried to put my arm around your shoulders, your entire face grew dark and cloudy.

If anything, it just made me want you more. I've had many women, Helena. They come to me at night, whether I'm living in the damp sand in Lagos or on some empty street outside *Lisboa*, near Praia do Gaucho. *Mas você é muito diferente.* When I find your glimmering eyes wandering across the crowded market. When I hear your faint knock on my door at night, almost as if you're still not sure. When we're sinking into the red sand under the overturned boat, pressing into each other. I can think of no one else, *meu amor*, no one else. After you lightly pad away in bare feet and disappear down the beach, I hear you in the swirl and lap of the water, the gray whisper of the sky at dawn, the scattering of sand in the breeze.

I want to take you away from here. I *need* to take you away. I want no one else, Helena, just you. And I'm going to tell you tonight, my love. *Estou nervoso! Onde está você?* I can show you how I live, how to drift from town to town. We only need each other. It sounds crazy, I know.

You say *seu noivo* Nuno loves you, and you love him. You've said that right along. But I don't care about him, and I don't believe you. The other night you told me that I made you feel things that you never have, as your fingers drew slow circles across the bare skin of my back and your two different eyes flickered like fireflies in the darkness.

Meu Deus! Por favor, venha depressa!

What if you don't come? What if you were lying? What if something happened to you? *Eu te amo,* Helena. I swear that I do. I said it last night in bed. You didn't say it back, but you nodded in the darkness. And I knew what you meant. I knew.

With each glass of wine I drink, the tide climbs a little higher. *Eu tea mo*, Helena. *Apprese-se*. The sun will rise soon.

where to?

You lie there, breathing very deliberately. "But if it happens tomorrow, how long will it take?"

The television buzzes behind me. It seems like they only show sitcoms here; half-hour segments steeped in canned laughter and oblivion. I step closer to the bed and squeeze your right foot. It's cold, even under the sheet. With my other hand I reach under my shirt and pinch the soft skin of my stomach to keep my voice level.

"It's not going to happen tomorrow or the day after, or the day after that," I fib. I pretend that we are talking about something else. A thunderstorm. A tooth falling out. I rub your toes until they feel warmer. "Not tomorrow or any other day. This is just a little vacation. Like when we went to Virginia, remember?"

"With the horses and the mini-golf and the hotel pool shaped like a peanut," you recite. "Right?"

I watch you close your eyes to send yourself back there, and I close mine, too. I remember lifting you onto my shoulders in the pool, spinning you around. And chasing each other, roaring with laughter, our wet feet slapping on the cold pavement while Hailey yelled for us to stop because someone could get hurt. But neither of us listened, and you whooped and hollered when I almost slipped and fell.

But it *had* been dangerous. And now I'm ashamed. It was irresponsible and careless. Maybe Hailey has been right all along. I open my eyes and stare carefully at your face, unsure whether you're asleep or not. You look nothing like the girl from that day anymore. Your face is not reddened by the sun and peppered with Hailey's light freckles, but sunken and pale.

Then you cough. It sounds like a piece of cardboard ripping.

Like a magnet my hand goes to your forehead. It scorches. I push the longer hairs back. Your breathing is definitely worse than it was yesterday, when I lied to Hailey in the hallway before she went in and told her that you weren't any worse; you weren't any better but you weren't any worse. She hadn't believed me anyway. The doctor had already told her the same thing he told me—that you could *pass* any day now. God, how I fucking hate that word *pass*.

"I want to sit up," you say.

I can feel the sharpness of your ribs, the dampness of your back sticking to the sheets. I push lumpy pillows behind you, moving one over to cover a yellowed stain on the wall. Footsteps clack down the hallway.

"Dad, I hate this place," you whisper. "I really hate it. I wish we could just . . . *go*."

That's all it takes.

It happens so fast: bringing the car around, flicking the hazard lights on and then striding quickly back. Running with you hanging over my shoulder, jostling against me, so lightweight and frail that you could crumble into pieces at any moment. Your laughter falling to the linoleum floor, sounding unnatural and guttural, in part because I haven't heard it in months and in part because you're hanging upside down. The nurse and the receptionist squawking and then actually running after us, the slamming of doors and the way you sink into the seat and smile up at me, as if we have all the time in the world.

I jam my Red Sox hat onto your head and you pull it down as sirens and car horns blast all around us. My arm locks you into place, and we swerve across the parking lot, gaining speed. You cling to my arm, the same arm that just swung and elbowed whoever was following us. I'd felt the soft give of flesh, heard a shocked gush of breath. *The police!* A woman had cried. *I'm calling the police! Security! Where is security?!*

But none of it matters to me. Assault, negligence, life, death. None of it.

"Where to, miss?" I ask, biting my lip and checking the rearview as we weave through traffic. It's an old game we used to play. You are the famous movie star.

Just don't say home, I think, *where Hailey's camped out, smoking Parliaments with her friends and blaming me for everything that's gone wrong this year. Please don't say home, Emily.*

"The beach?"

"As you wish."

And then we're there.

It is September, clear and empty at East Matunuck. You're shivering as I carry you down the path we always take, the tall grass licking at my legs, sharp. When we can see the water, I cheer and feel your grasp tighten. The waves lap quietly at the shore and glint with the gray shine of autumn.

I kneel and sit down next to an empty lifeguard chair, resting my back on the worn wooden slats. You curl up on my chest. Your breathing actually sounds better. I rub your back and cover us in the blanket I grabbed out of the trunk. You squirm until comfortable and sigh. After a few moments I shut my eyes, too.

I don't mean to fall asleep. I haven't slept well in months, though. I haven't actually *slept* in about a week. There's no one else at the beach that day—no eager shouts of children or loose chatter of adults to wake us. There is only the beating of your heart, light and fast, and the slow whisper of the waves.

"Dad?" you say. "Dad?"

I blink and watch you stand and stretch, your face glowing in the stiff wind, the gold and red of sunset. "Emily? What—"

"I feel better!" you shout. "I'm better!" And you do a little skipping dance down to the water's edge, the same dance that you used to do at the breakfast table, your socks sliding on the linoleum floor, your hands clutching a pen that you pretended was a microphone.

The tide is low, and the wet sand sticks to my sneakers as I follow you. You wade into the dark water up to your thighs, still dancing. Your white hospital gown ripples around your slight body in the wind, and my red hat is perched on your head.

"Emily!" I call, striding into the water. "Come back! Emily!"

You giggle and only wave back at me. "I love you, Dad," you holler as you splash in deeper. A few seconds pass, and then my hat surfaces and I thrash toward it, thinking that you're under it, but a wave breaks against my waist and my hands come up floundering, empty. You're way further out now, slipping under the waves with ease—*Where are you going?* Chest deep, I run and dive after you, my hands slashing the cold surface. But you cry out and then disappear under another curling sheet of water, the bottoms of your feet pink beneath the white, then gone.

"Emily!" I scream, "Emily!" The dying sunlight shimmers across the surface. For a moment, I can still hear your voice, echoing with the waves.

They find me curled up under the lifeguard chair the next morning. I'm still wet, chilled to the bone. Hailey's face slides in and out, her teeth flashing. I want to stand up and grab her cheeks with both hands and rip that look off her face, but I can't. Instead, I sit there, unable to move. The muscles in my arms and legs are numb. The thin bones of my face are heavy. I listen to the ragged cries as they grow faint and swirl in the wind. I watch Hailey scratch my face and get pulled away. The sheriff looks at me with what is either pity or disappointment. I can't tell which.

—

That's all I can remember. I could never answer the questions that anyone asked me—my family, my friends, that awful, patronizing shrink—anyone. I could never tell a story that they believed, and after a while I gave up.

When I decided to leave, I knew you'd come with me, Emily. Tonight, I can feel you in the empty seat next to me as the plane trembles and then takes off against the cold winter wind. This is your first time on a plane, and together we watch the lights of Boston smolder in the sky and then begin to bleed into the ocean. I'm not sure either of us will ever see them again.

I've never told anyone what you called out to me right before you dove under for the last time, Emily. I've never admitted to the things that we still talk about. Sometimes I wait all night and you never arrive. Other times you are there waiting for me when I close my eyes. You beg me to hoist you up on my shoulders and swing you around. Of course, I oblige. The stars cast blurry lines across the sky as we spin, the ocean surges and beckons us. You hold on tightly, laughing, urging me to keep going.

But the night never lasts long enough, does it?

portuguese in the americas series

Portuguese-Americans and Contemporary
Civic Culture in Massachusetts
Edited by Clyde W. Barrow

Through a Portagee Gate
Charles Reis Felix

In Pursuit of Their Dreams:
A History of Azorean
Immigration to the United States
Jerry R. Williams

Sixty Acres and a Barn · Alfred Lewis

Da Gama, Cary Grant, and the Election
of 1934 · Charles Reis Felix

Distant Music · Julian Silva

Representations of the Portuguese
in American Literature · Reinaldo Silva

The Holyoke · Frank X. Gaspar

Two Portuguese-American Plays
Paulo A. Pereira and Patricia A. Thomas
Edited by Patricia A. Thomas

Tony: A New England Boyhood
Charles Reis Felix

Community, Culture and The Makings
of Identity: Portuguese-Americans Along
the Eastern Seaboard · Edited by
Kimberly DaCosta Holton
and Andrea Klimt

The Undiscovered Island · Darrell Kastin

So Ends This Day: The Portuguese in
American Whaling 1765–1927
Donald Warrin

Azorean Identity in Brazil and the United
States:Arguments about History, Culture,
and Transnational Connections
João Leal · Translated by Wendy Graça

Move Over, Scopes and Other Writings
Julian Silva

The Marriage of the Portuguese
(Expanded Edition) · Sam Pereira

Home Is an Island · Alfred Lewis

Land of Milk and Money
Anthony Barcellos

The Conjurer and Other Azorean Tales
Darrell Kastin